Shadow of Fear

Shadow of Fear

A Novel

Gilmer White

Copyright ©2017 Gilmer White
ISBN 978-0-9992500-2-0
All rights reserved under
International and Pan-American Copyright

Published by Low Country Press
Savannah, Georgia
www.lowcountrypress.net

Library of Congress Cataloging-in-Publication Data
is available on request.

Manufactured in the United States of America

First Edition: August 2017
9 8 7 6 5 4 3 2 1

DEDICATION

I dedicate this book to Victoria Steele Logue,
friend, editor, and fellow writer.

ACKNOWLEDGEMENTS

For my wife JoAnn for keeping me grounded during rough times when words would not come.

For Mary Catherine, my sister, my best friend.

For dear friends Victoria and Frank Logue who have kept the faith that all writers need.

For good friend Kim Garrigan Jones who inspires me.

For my publisher, Low Country Press, whose design and editing work is remarkable.

For Barbara and Jim [Bud] Dunn, friends forever.

For Michael Fatula, for his friendship and continuing support for my writing.

For Jon Peterson, friend and early supporter of my writing and his wife Marie who knows a thing or two about cooking.

For Robert Ulm, friend and fellow dog lover.

For John Spires, motivator and inspirer.

Maris Cato, for interest and insight.

For my classmates and friends at The University of the South, Sewanee, TN [ECCE QUAM BONUM].

And finally, to all whom I have missed who have enjoyed my writing, I thank you.

In memoriam: Janet Finkelstein, beloved feisty member of our original writers' group, Ink In Our Veins.

PREFACE

The author was a child in the 1930's. His style of writing is colored by that relatively tranquil period before World War II, characterized among many other things by an absence of television, where we sat before hump-back heavy radios driven by hot vacuum tubes, with most entertainment at home primarily from books and magazines; or if you were a very young child as I was, stories, often exaggerated for effect, told by Mom or Dad. My writing has that stamp. At heart, I am essentially a storyteller, my writing lacking the embellishment essential to longer pieces of fiction, but not to a storyteller. *Shadow of Fear* was written in that fashion. It is the second book in a modern gothic trilogy, *A Time Before the End* being the first, and *Ashes on the Wind*, not yet completed, to be the third. Many of the characters from *A Time before the End* have found their way into *Shadow of Fear*, but it is not necessary for the reader to have read my earlier book as I have

Shadow of Fear

written *Shadow of Fear* as a story to stand on its own. The title is taken from lines in T.S. Eliot's poem *The Waste Land*:

> Come in under the shadow of this red rock,
> And I will show you something different from either
> Your shadow at morning striding behind you
> Or your shadow at evening rising to meet you;
> I will show you fear in a handful of dust.

PART ONE

JOURNEY INTO TERROR

PROLOGUE

I am Mary. That's all I go by now—just Mary. Although my family calls me Mary Celeste, I have also gone by other names: Postulant, Novice, Sister, Bride of Christ, Mother Superior, and even some names like Adulteress and Whore. I will let you decide what you wish to think of me.

I came here to the Outer Banks of North Carolina with the child born in my forty-fifth year to get away from the national attention and sort out the debris of my life. It's a long and solitary journey from my hometown of Hanover, North Carolina, to Highway 12 near Manteo on Roanoke Island, the site of the Lost Colony. A right turn takes you across the fierce Oregon Inlet onto Hatteras Island for the 58-mile trip to the small fishing village of Hatteras itself. That's the last stop. That's where you will find me.

I live in a wooden house, both small and old, and beaten by the storms of sixty years. It stands on a narrow, shell-littered, sandy road along with three old, weathered, and deserted rentals separated in a random fashion as if location was a second thought. The road runs into a barrier thirty yards away from my home, and beyond that there is a sand dune crowned with sea oats, and finally the ocean. I thought I would be here for just a short time, but the old house has had its way with me and I have remained.

Today, with a northeaster raking the coast, and the bleakness of winter casting its pall over the Outer Banks, the child and I are inside huddled next to an ancient, wood-burning stove of cast iron. Sitting, there, we can see through a break in the dunes to the angry sea beyond. I thrust a few pieces of wind-twisted firewood into the stove, bring the child close to me, and wrap the two of us in a blanket; and I think, I think, about another child, one taken from me, and all that has gone before.

It seems my life has always been wrapped around the turbulence of wind and water, as I was born not far from the mouth of the Cape Fear River with its fearsome name and destructive reality. I was the youngest of what would have been four, but two miscarriages separated me from my older sister Sarah by ten years. What happened to her, and the Porter family into which she married, should have given me pause about the other side of religious fervor, but few believed in what was then rumored to be a curse upon a house and family. Even now, so many years later, I wonder if somehow the curse attached itself to me.

Our family came from a long line of the faithful and went to Mass every Sunday, on feast days, and even on special occasions; but I can't say you would call us devout in the sense of having crucifixes, icons, paintings of the Holy Mother and Child, and rosaries on display for all who entered our home. Our house was bare of these symbols.

I was different from the rest of my family. I became captured at an early age by the beauty of holiness that I found in these very objects, and in the intimacy felt when I stood before the altar and looked up at the Crucifix and sculptures of the Saints on their pedestals. The priests and nuns always gave me special attention so I was not entirely surprised when one chilly afternoon close to my seventeenth birthday, two nuns arrived at our home. They were just visiting some shut-ins who lived nearby, the Pelham's and Tucker's, and decided to stop by to discuss something they had been meaning to talk to my parents about.

What did my parents think about Mary Celeste continuing her education after high school in a convent program that would prepare her for a vocation that would serve the Church? My parents were practically speechless and turned to me. I smiled and said I would think about it. One of the nuns handed my parents some literature, and the two left.

That's the way my story starts. When I took my final vows of poverty, chastity, and obedience, my parents cried. They thought I was too young and pretty to be a nun. Eventually I went to teach at a parochial school located in the intercity of New Orleans on the grounds with St. Benedict's church and the convent of Sisters of the Holy Supplication. I was so happy doing what God wanted for me—until I met Father Vincent Gower, and a shadow of fear was cast upon my life.

THE FAIREST
OF THEM ALL

Father Vincent Gower's haggard face and ragged mop of prematurely grey hair gave him the appearance of a saint emerging from the desert after forty days of praying and fasting. Despite the raging emotions gnawing at the razor edge of his consciousness, he seemed to have a sincere face, one that was humble and ready to hear a confession and give absolution. If you were to crawl through the twisted conch-like passages of Vincent's brain, you might find yourself able to capture the essence of his agony, but there would be no guarantee.

All of the signposts pointed in a different direction, but Vincent was convinced he knew what he wanted in life and had felt the fulfillment tantalizingly within his grasp several times. Then, like a greased pig, it slipped away, and he was left depressed and resentful. As a result, Vincent felt he had been driven to do things that sometimes got him into trouble and reassigned from one parish to another, usually in another diocese. But he was still young. He had time.

Shadow of Fear

Vincent had been at St. Benedict's just a short time—hardly long enough to get settled—when Father Dolan suffered a severe stroke. He was only sixty-four, but he was left with both his facial and leg muscles crippled on the left side of his body. Word traveled quickly through the grapevine that he wasn't coming back. Someone else would soon be assigned.

In the interim, Vincent would be in charge, and by default have a final chance to prove he wasn't just a "dead cat" being thrown over the wall from one parish to another. A vision stood before his eyes like a beacon on a foggy night: a parish of his own over which he had absolute control. Situated in an almost forgotten part of New Orleans where poverty and crime reigned, it was a parish the Bishop rarely visited. The situation was perfect for Vincent's presence to be felt throughout the area. He would be the person the lost in society came to for help. They would be his sheep, and he would be their shepherd. In view of the totality of what happened later, the vision he had for himself didn't scratch the surface.

For Vincent, one of the main attractions of St. Benedict's campus, as it was known, was a school taught by nuns from an adjacent convent led by an old Mother Superior who believed in the preeminence of priests and was deferential to their wishes. It was just the kind of setup Vincent was looking for. There were even a few attractive nuns among the Sisters of the Holy Supplication, and Sister Mary Celeste was the fairest of them all. In fact, Vincent thought, she was downright beautiful with a figure even a habit couldn't hide, and she gave the impression of being naïve and oh so innocent. Were there still women out there who walked in beauty like an angel? Vincent's passions were inflamed to the point they boiled over, and his imagination filled with the most sinful of acts.

Sister Mary Celeste was a teacher at the parochial school, and on one of New Orleans' rare mild days, she was sitting on a bench reading some test papers when Vincent sat down beside her.

"I'm Vincent Gower," he said simply.

"Hello Father," she said shyly. "I'm Sister Mary Celeste. I heard you preach on Sunday. We were all moved."

He laughed. "It was one of the congregation's favorites from my old parish," he said, an Irish lilt on his tongue. "Thought I'd get off on the right foot."

Mary Celeste smiled the neutral smile one sees in the afternoon when waiting to be served tea. "Well, it's certainly nice to meet you. We have a lot of young people here whom I think will identify with you."

And that's the way their pivotal first meeting went—friendly, but not too personal—all about St. Benedict's and the school.

Their next meeting was in the school library when Vincent sat down beside her, a little too close, she thought, but then, how else could one talk in the library? Just a short greeting, an intense peering into her face, a somewhat intimate smile, and he was gone. But Vincent wasn't really gone. Mary Celeste continued to feel his presence in the halls of the school, around the campus as she was walking, and in religious ceremonies where she felt his proximity pressing on her boundaries as if she had been placed in a vise.

The example she could best articulate was her spiritual work with contemplative prayer in sessions that Father Dolan had been leading. During these sessions, the nuns practiced the Lectio Divina, or divine reading, the traditional Benedictine practice of scriptural reading, meditation, prayer, and contemplation intended to help one come into closer communion with God. After Father Dolan's stroke, Vincent took over the sessions. Mary Celeste felt trapped when on the first session Vincent squeezed in the pew between her and another nun. As he asked Mary Celeste to recount her experience with the practice, she could feel him pressing against her, his breath laced with mouthwash and hot on her cheek. But there was one traumatic experience that stood out from all the rest.

As Mary Celeste later told her spiritual advisor: "I can't believe how naïve I was back then. I truly wanted to think Father Vincent's intentions were honorable, and did until one day when Mother Therese instructed me to accompany him on a visit to a shut-in to offer her the sacrament of the Mass. As her address was located at the far end of the 9th Ward, we took Father Dolan's old

Buick and drove to a run-down section inhabited mostly by people of African and Creole descent. We arrived at a small bungalow where an old black lady sat in a rocker with a shawl over her lap. At her feet lay an old, spotted dog that raised his head and growled as we approached.

"'Hush, Lenny,' the old woman said. The dog dropped his head. 'If you haven't seen one before,' she told us, 'he's a Catahoula Leopard Dog, recognized as the State dog of Louisiana. Got too old for hunting, and I took him in before they could put him down.'

"She was very dignified. She had been, she told us, a teacher in New York when she was younger. She returned years ago to serve her people. Well, after the Mass was concluded, she offered us tea, but Father Vincent declined saying we had another stop to make. That surprised me because he hadn't brought it up before. When we were back in the car he said he wanted to visit a famous old cemetery with a chapel on the grounds that someone had told him about. The cemetery had been there forever, but the chapel had been constructed in the Eighteenth Century, and many healing miracles were reported there during the yellow fever and black plague epidemics of those times.

"It was late in the afternoon when we arrived, and the cemetery was spooky with above ground crypts and graves that had caved in. Ancient oak trees threw dark shadows everywhere. Father Vincent placed his hand on my shoulder and led me as if I were blind through a maze of headstones until we reached a small fenced in area with a rusted, sagging gate with a sign that said 'no trespassing.'

"'I was told about this,' he told me. 'It's a burial plot for poor souls said to be haunted by demons—those unable to be helped by the Church performing an exorcism.' He then pointed to a sign. 'Look at the inscription posted on the gate. It's from an ancient litany taken from a Scottish book of prayers.'

"The sign read: From ghoulies and ghosties and long-leggedy beasties, and things that go bump in the night, Good Lord deliver us.'

"Father Vincent tugged at the gate, which made a horrible squeak. It reminded me of chalk on a blackboard, and my nerve endings tingled. Despite the warning on the gate, he pulled me inside. I could see that some of the headstones were so old and worn from time and the elements that they could hardly be read. Father seemed intrigued by several and knelt before one and took out his handkerchief and began to dust it off. Just then, we heard an urgent voice behind us.

"'Father, don't touch the headstones.'

"There, peering at us over smudged spectacles stood the old hump-shouldered caretaker for the cemetery. He was pushing a wheelbarrow filled with gardening tools and trimmings, and staring at us as if he were seeing demons.

"'You and Sister shouldn't be in there,' he said, and his voice quivering. 'They say bad things happen to those who enter. Demons, I hear.'

"But, Father Vincent continued cleaning the inscription on the headstone until he could make out the writing. 'Joshua Barrow, 1725-1773,' he read. 'Died from a broken neck while sleeping. God watch over ye. Good Lord," he said, and he turned to face the caretaker. 'How do they know demons are responsible?'

"The caretaker kept staring at us. He seemed nervous, and his jaw kept moving as he worked on a plug of tobacco.

"'They say Church keep records, that's all I know,' he told us, and then said, ''cept all them in that place die in a bad way with broken necks and things like that while they be alone. I'd move along if I was you.'

"Father Vincent checked a few more headstones, and I could see the puzzlement on his face as he retreated from the gravesite and we and moved on to the chapel. An old attendant opened the door and we walked in and started to read from plaques about the people who founded this chapel and those who attended during a dark period in the history of New Orleans.

"I was concentrating on trying to follow the narrative when I felt a tug on the veil I wore covering my head. It had been pulled back to reveal the top of my head. At the time my hair had been cropped short because of the heat and humidity, and I felt naked.

"'I had to see what you looked like without the veil,' Vincent whispered into my ear.

"No man had ever seen me without head cover since I was a postulant. I felt horribly violated.

"I was overcome by anger, and that was an emotion I seldom felt at that time in my life. I turned to face him, and I fixed my eyes directly on his. 'Father Vincent, you have no right to do that,' I cried.

"He bowed his head pretending to be a naughty student suddenly reprimanded by his teacher. "'I'm attracted by your beauty,' he said. 'You must know that by now.'

"I felt his breath on my head, and I backed away. 'What you're doing is violating your vows,' I told him. 'You must leave me alone or I'll have to report you to Mother Superior.' I tried to say it in the most intimidating voice I could muster.

Father Vincent must have felt the heat of my anger. He managed a brief crooked smile. 'Mother Therese listens first to priests so I would advise you against that,' he told me, 'but please accept my heartfelt apology.' He said it with a wink and slowly walked away. I'm sure the repulsion showed on my face. I had heard stories of Mother Superiors who turned their backs while priests took their pleasure with nuns. I had made very few decisions for myself since I had taken vows, but I knew now I must make an important one. When I got back to my room, I prayed that I would make the right one."

BERSERK

Vincent Gower's Irish face burned red, and his visage was as distorted as if a mound of clay had been sculpted into some grotesque, gargoyle shape. Enraged, he swept his hand across the desk scattering papers and objects everywhere. He stomped and cursed until Carol, the parish secretary, opened the door to check on him. Upon seeing the room and Vincent's twisted face, she raised her hands to her eyes to blot out the scene.

"Get out! Get Out!" Vincent screamed. A terrified Carol ran from the room crying. Once again, Vincent had gone berserk!

The man in the purple vestments had warned Vincent about his mood swings, and the potential danger to others. After one publically frightening episode, the Bishop had to send him away. Vincent had been forced to take the medication prescribed, and the rehabilitation at the Church's estate-like facility near the sea.

After his mania had been brought under control, he was released to the Bishop, and soon was transferred to a new diocese, and finally to the church at St Benedicts surrounded as it was by poverty and awash with crime. Surely, Vincent could control himself in that environment.

One might ask what would cause this kind of aberrant behavior in a "man of the cloth"? Offended Pride in all its omnipotence?

Ambition brought to no good end? Music of the soul squelched before its time? A mere hint should be enough.

Vincent had just gotten off the phone with Bishop Brennan of the diocese. After some awkward small talk, the Bishop got to the point. He had selected someone other than Vincent to be priest-in-charge of St. Benedict's. Father Keitel was coming. Vincent had been introduced to him at a diocesan meeting—an austere looking German Jesuit priest who didn't seem to have a humorous bone in his body. And Vincent was supposed to kowtow to him? That would be the day!

"Your plan for working with the people in your Ward is far more important than managing the day to day details of the parish. Please keep me up-to-date on your progress," the Bishop had said, ending the conversation.

When he had stopped trembling with rage, Vincent stomped out of the parish office. He began to walk aimlessly along the sidewalks and trails that bisected the church and school property, head down, fuming as he went. He needed a higher purpose for his life than playing second fiddle to a jerk like Keitel. Practically everyone said Vincent was a great author and preacher. A number of his sermons and columns for the Religion section of local newspapers, along with an embellished Introduction describing the path of his journey as a priest, had been gathered and published as a book entitled *Pathway to Jesus.* Not to mention the fact that he had just recently been referred to in an article as "the handsome, charismatic Father Vincent Gower."

What more did the Bishop want? What more did the Church want for that matter? Hadn't he long sought a larger role in the life of the Church than the one he had as a parish priest? Unfortunately, whenever his ambitions had been frustrated, something began to churn inside of him—that old familiar feeling he had learned to dread. It was an obsession he could not shut down, one that took over his will power and drove him against everything he professed— a burning, carnal desire for the beautiful women who surrounded him.

Without realizing it, Vincent arrived at the convent. He had to see Mother Therese and Mary Celeste before they found out he wasn't going to be the priest-in-charge any more. He knew Mary Celeste was mad about what happened two days ago, but felt sure she would understand once he explained. He was creating a scenario to explain it all as he climbed the twelve steps, and rapped with the heavy iron knocker on the oak door. Time passed. He knocked again. Finally the door cracked to reveal a squat nun in full habit with the build of a sumo wrestler.

"Yes?" she asked, her eyes fixed on him like a hawk on a rabbit.

"I'm looking for Mother Superior and Sister Mary Celeste," he said. "I missed Sister at our Lectio Divina meeting yesterday. I thought something might be wrong."

"I'm sorry, Father Vincent," she said abruptly. "Sister Mary is not available; neither is the Mother Superior. I can't confide any other details."

Vincent cursed under his breath. He had been riding so high, and now to be rudely brought down to earth. The death knell to his ambitions in the Church was as obvious as an angry slap on the face. Mary Celeste's not being available only added to his humiliation. It was apparent she had told Mother Superior how he was pursuing her, and had won her over with the testimony of other nuns who weren't blind to what was happening.

It occurred to Vincent to ask the question, and in his vivid imagination create the answer: What was the limited future remaining for him in the Church? Perhaps it was as priest-in-charge of a small rural church in Mississippi where if his eyes remained for too long on the bosoms of their wives and daughters, who were exposing as much of themselves as possible against the torrid summer heat, their redneck husbands or fathers would take Vincent out in the woods behind the church without asking questions; or some remote parish in Alaska where the Inuit women were not his type.

All that was really left to his fantasy was Mary Celeste. He had to win her sympathy, and perhaps that would open a door for him. If she'd left the convent, someone on campus would know. He checked with security. A car rental agency had sent a van to pick her up. A telephone log, which both the clergy and nuns were required to keep, revealed a call to a location near Hanover, North Carolina, her home town. Finding out where her family's property was located would be easy, and Vincent had access to a retired priest who filled in when the church needed him. Out of control, and unable to restrain himself, Vincent packed quickly and left.

Vincent drove the gas-guzzling, oil burning, twelve-year-old coupe he had driven in his transfers from diocese to diocese down a narrow macadam road which ended abruptly at the driveway of a home with a pier in back that had a boathouse at the end. The house was located on a body of water that ran swiftly to an inlet that emptied into the ocean a few miles away.

There was a plumbing repair truck in front. A short, skinny man who looked as if he could fit into any tight spot manueved a washing machine on a dolly. It wasn't safe to stop, but Vincent had to find out if Mary Celeste was there. He stuck his head out the window.

"Is anyone home?" Vincent asked.

The short man craned his neck to look at Vincent.

"There was a woman here, but she rode her bike back towards the highway. Said she wouldn't be gone long. If her sister came, she'd be over at the beach."

Vincent retraced his route up the macadam road to Highway A1A. On the other side was a shell road with a sign that read "Beach Entry." At the end of the entry was a path through the sand dunes to the beach. The leather–soled shoes that Vincent wore at church slipped on the fine sand as he struggled to gain traction. His level of frustration rose as he exerted himself to reach a point where he would have a clear view of the strand. He squinted to see any movement, making out what others might miss. Finally, far down the beach toward the inlet he spied a solitary figure riding a bike on the hard packed sand left by the retreating surf.

The weather was beginning to deteriorate as clouds built over the ocean. There was no one else in sight. Vincent returned to his car and drove down the shell road until he came to a small motel that had once been a retreat for out-of-town fishermen who came to the area to fish during the red drum season, but was now abandoned. He parked his car in front where it could not be seen from the beach.

Mist had now begun to roll in from the ocean and visibility was poor, but when Vincent walked to a cut between the dunes, he could see Mary Celeste coming toward him pushing a bike. She had shed her clothing from the convent and was wearing pedal pushers and a pull-over against the increasing chill. A baseball cap covered her hair but Vincent knew what it looked like underneath. He was transfixed. Coming up the path was the woman he desired, the one about whom he'd spent numerous nights fantasizing, and she was headed straight for the motel and him.

DEFILED

I always surprise myself when I unlock the door of my memory to face events of the past. Surprised because I never thought I'd be like I am now. It is as if I had lived in a cocoon most of my life—protected and nourished by the Church—as I slowly prepared to emerge as a beautiful butterfly. But the butterfly I was to become, never emerged. Or, if it did it, it was not the one that I, or anyone else, expected.

Mother Superior, in her compassion, gave me a leave of absence to visit my family in North Carolina after the period of tribulation caused by Father Gower. One day in April while I was visiting my sister and brother-in-law, I decided to take one of their bicycles for a ride on the beach near their home.

The weather was still trying to make up its mind about whether to be pleasant or not. I set out on a day that seemed spring-like, but which turned rather nasty as a rain cloud blew in from the east, and I was forced to seek shelter. Fortunately, I was familiar with my surroundings, and headed for a deserted motel that sat just off the ocean. It had once been a popular destination for fishermen and the occasional tourist, but when the State decided to change the direction of the highway, it slowly lost its clientele and eventually closed.

It's also strange how memory sometimes has a perverse appeal, enticing you, and then like a mother pulling a child, leading you in a direction you had rather not go to a place forbidden in memory itself. I had spent time in this motel before when I was a teenager.

My older sister, Sarah, had gone to live with Ben Porter who had recently returned from the war. He was managing this motel at a time when horrible things happened in it. Sarah had been raped, and that monster, Luther, had kidnapped Ben's daughter, Rachel. So, was it by chance that I chose this particular location to seek shelter from the rain or was there some other force at work?

I pushed my bike up onto the cracked blacktop of the parking area, leaving it on its side, and headed towards what had once been a lobby. The door had been smashed in and then propped up. Beer cans and food bags littered the floor. I remember now that in one corner was a small, burned out charcoal grill with its greasy contents on the floor. Several soiled mattresses had been dragged in and positioned near a wood fireplace. The transient inhabitants had not stayed long enough to clean up, and one messy scene had become just another layer of debris.

Now, standing there in the midst of it all with memories creeping in like sly intruders, a foreboding of terror came over me and I began to shudder. The room suddenly grew very cold, and I became aware of a human presence even though I could see nothing.

"Hello Mary Celeste," a voice said.

From the shadows in the far corner, which had once housed a drink machine, Father Vincent Gower stepped forward. He was dressed in khakis, a sports shirt, and light sweater. He held a bag in one hand that sagged from the weight of whatever it held. A crooked smile crossed his face, and I knew I was in trouble.

"Father Vincent, what are you doing here?" I said, and slowly backed towards the door.

"You mustn't try to leave, Mary. I came to tell you something."

"You shouldn't be here. You know that!"

"I have to be," he said. "I'm leaving the priesthood. Bishop Brennan has appointed someone else to lead St. Benedict's and I have no future there now, especially if I could not see you. So I have to be here to talk to you, to beg you not to shut me out."

"Father Vincent, you know I can't have a personal relationship with you, if that's what you want. You're a gifted man. I urge you to return to St. Benedict's and take your place. Accept your new responsibilities whatever they may be."

I took a small step backwards, inching my way toward the outside door of the lobby. He moved slowly towards me, the hand with the bag outstretched.

His voice took on a hard edge. "You must not shun me like this," he said.

"I'm sorry," I said quietly so as not to enrage him further and continued to back toward the door.

Father Vincent moved quickly, the paper bag now discarded to reveal a metal device that resembled a poker with a small box attached. I turned to run and that's when I felt the shock that turned my legs to rubber and paralyzed my throat muscles.

I was sitting on the floor convulsing when he picked me up and laid me on one of the filthy mattresses. He pulled off my clothing and got on top of me. He stole my innocence.

The effect of the shock was wearing off, and I began to struggle and push him away. In the process of becoming a nun I had forgotten that one of my physical attributes was strength, and he was having difficulty holding me down.

"You don't want me, do you, do you?" Vincent cried out. "Well, when I finish with you, neither God nor man will ever want to look at you again."

Did I see a flash of steel? A terrible pain seared the left side of my face, and when I moved my head, I felt something warm on my skin and saw blood. I felt the pain again, this time in my left breast, which he had grasped. I tried to scream. Finally the sound came.

His hand covered my mouth. "Shut up, shut up!" he hissed between gritted teeth and he raised his fist. That's all I remembered until I heard a voice nearby.

"Wha . . . what happened here lady? You need to get to a hospital fast!"

It was a homeless man looking for a place to spend the night. A second man with a grimy beard came over and looked down at my nude, bleeding body.

"Maybe we need to get out of here," he said.

"Naw, we can't do that," the first one said. "Wouldn't be right. I'll take that bike outside and go get help. You help her get her clothes back on, but keep your hands off, hear me!"

"Oh, God, look what someone has done to her," a trauma room nurse said.

"Did they find the ear and part of the breast?" one of the doctors asked without emotion. "It hasn't been that long. We could try to reattach them."

"No. The emergency team looked all over the place. Whoever did it must have taken them," the first nurse said.

"Sweet Jesus," the other nurse said.

MAN IN PURPLE

Vincent stood before the rustic teak door of an antebellum home in the historic district of Charleston, South Carolina. To his rear lay the famous Battery, the once fortified seawall at the southernmost tip of the Charleston peninsula.

Vincent could hardly believe what had happened hundreds of miles away at the dilapidated motel in the North Carolina's outer banks. In the past he had avoided punishment with the help of the church, but this time was different. His actions would cost him dearly even if he could elude the manhunt that would soon be tracking him. He remembered almost running over two men as he fled the motel. They appeared to be vagabonds as they were carrying cardboard suitcases, and they were headed for the broken door of what once had been a lobby.

"There's a woman inside who's hurt. Get help quick!" Vincent had yelled, and sped away. He drove carefully staying well within the speed limit. He didn't want to risk drawing attention to his car, which he realized would no doubt be reported by the homeless men he'd nearly run down. He stopped in a crowded rest area to wait until darkness crept in before he drove south to the home of the person also known as the Ancient One.

Vincent quickly approached the arched door and rang the bell. He could hear the chimes inside and in a moment the outside light came on, and a voice issued through the speaker. "May I help you," someone with a soft, accented voice said.

"Saint Kevin calls," Vincent said, intoning the secret password. It referred to the Irish Saint who established a monastery in the 6th Century at Glendalough, Ireland, where Vincent's brother had a small church. It was a code to use only in case of a dire emergency.

The door opened to reveal a large black man whose soft, almost feminine voice didn't seem to match. "My name is Lewis," the man said. "I believe the Bishop is expecting you. Please follow me."

Walking through the foyer and down a hall, the two soon came to a door upon which Lewis knocked before stepping back and standing behind Vincent.

The door was opened to reveal a very old man dressed with a white clerical collar and a purple pleated shirt. On his right hand was a large, ornate bishop's ring. His hoary appearance startled Vincent. How could this man have walked with his own father in the Easter Rising quest for independence in Ireland?

"Your transgression is all over the news," the Bishop said. "I take it your car is in the drive."

Vincent nodded. The ancient man turned to his servant. "Lewis, get rid of it even if it takes all night. Take it over to the island and have some of your family dismantle it and lose the parts or whatever they want to do as long as it disappears for good. But wait until I'm finished with Vincent. You'll be taking him with you." He turned back toward Vincent, explaining, "Lewis was born on one of the nearby barrier islands in a Gullah community and speaks the dialect. Vincent, please give him your keys and come into my study."

The Ancient One seated himself in a plain, cushioned rocker before looking up at Vincent, who stood. "If I had been wise, I would not have admitted you. You have done a terrible thing, and if it were not for my relationship and allegiance to your father, you would not be standing where you are. You understand that even though I am retired from an active role in the Church, I still serve in many ways, and everything I stand for is at stake."

Many years ago, the Ancient One was at the Vatican as a trusted advisor to the Pontiff who sent him to Washington as a special emissary. The reason for this assignment was never revealed, but he had remained in the States where he soon became a Bishop in a diocese that needed a stern hand to guide it. When he retired to Charleston's exclusive Battery area with its scenic promenade and historic park, he chose a home estimated to be worth in the millions. Some people wondered where the money came from, but the Bishop had ingratiated himself to Charleston's high society where questions of wealth were in the worst of taste, and the curious soon turned their attention elsewhere.

The Bishop paused to reflect before he spoke again. "But yes, I will aid you, Vincent. My generation still has a few left who remember what loyalty is. I will bring someone to you who will attend to all the details of a new identity and getting you to Ireland. Your brothers will be alerted and expecting you. But in the meantime, we will protect you. You will not have an easy transition to safety in a new life, but you must take it if you wish to survive." Vincent left with Lewis to live with the inhabitants of a deserted rice plantation in a remote part of the low country near Charleston. He was quick to learn the techniques of weaving baskets from sweetgrass and constructing hammocks by hand from hemp. His longish grey hair had been shorn, and his body was so tanned he could be mistaken for the native Creoles selling their wares along the route north from Charleston to Pawley's Island, South Carolina. And as he mastered the Gullah dialect, and added his rhetorical skills, he became a big attraction for tourists. But when the Ancient One heard of it, he knew it was time for Vincent to leave for Ireland. Vincent was ready for the next stage of his life.

THE FUGITIVE

The small trawler plowed its way through the mounting, white-crested waves caused by the approaching storm to the north. The wind, picking up force, swept the Irish Sea like a giant broom, propelling stinging bullets of chilling rain before it. The two men standing at the helm braced themselves against the cruelty of the force about to hit them. The small port of Wicklow, Ireland, was still sixteen miles away. Reaching it would be a welcome finish to their voyage from England.

The man steering the boat turned a resigned face towards his passenger. He had heard the charges against his younger brother, and was concerned for his escape from the clutches of the law more than anything else.

"Our brother will be impatient now that we are not there on time," said Thomas Gower, a fisherman, and sometimes trafficker of forbidden cargo when crossing the Irish Sea was imperative. Vincent Gower, standing next to him laughed. "I see time has not improved his disposition," he said.

Kevin Gower, their older brother had been named after Saint Kevin. He was a priest at a small church adjoining the monastery's additional restorations, including Saint Kevin's Kitchen and the Church of Saint Mary, one of the earliest and best restored. At the precise moment of his brothers' comments, Kevin was preparing a stew of lamb, potatoes, onions, and greens grown from a small garden at the rear of the cottage that served as his rectory. Kevin had also withdrawn from the cellar an ample supply of claret with which to wash the meal down.

Nearly two hours late, and fearing his older brother's indignant response to the delay, not to mention his reaction to the news from the Bishop, Vincent reluctantly banged the heavy rapper against the door of the rectory. The homecoming, however, was not quite as expected. When the door opened, Kevin stepped forward, peering into the deteriorating weather. He squinted at Vincent as if what he had recently discovered about him had changed his perception of his brother. But Kevin had already decided not to spoil the brothers' reunion that as it had been many years since they'd last been together.

"Ah, the prodigal son has returned, I see," he proclaimed in a loud voice as he pulled both brothers into a small living area. It was obvious he would be in total control of the evening as he turned toward his other brother.

"And Thomas, where have you been?" he said. "Cavorting with the ladies or plying your scandalous trade at sea, or both?"

Thomas, who was in his late forties, and trying to both remain a bachelor and stay out of jail, grinned. "Better not to comment in your presence, Kevin," he said.

The brothers all roared, and looked at each other with delight as if they had just recovered a lost treasure. After wine, dinner, cigars, and conversation of no real consequence, Vincent and Thomas made pallets on the floor, and the three brothers retired for the evening.

At daylight the next morning Kevin and Vincent walked along the crooked stone pathway to the Church. The small building was more than a century old. Made of stone with wooden arches, redolent of wood smoke from a fireplace in a corner of the nave, it was the perfect place for what was to happen. Before entering, Kevin placed his hand on Vincent's shoulder. He turned him around so they were facing each other. Kevin's piercing blue eyes were as cold as ice, his distress so palpable it rested in the air between them. He would speak his mind before crossing the threshold into the sacred space.

"Vincent, I have heard from our family friend, the Ancient One, of your barbaric assault on one of our nuns, not only a sexual attack but a disfigurement. What in God's name is going on with you? What has led you to violate your vows, and trample on the commandments? You better have some answers for me."

Without another word the brothers entered the church. Shivering from the cold in the unheated structure, they took seats facing each other with no screen between them.

"Forgive me, Father, for I have sinned, by my fault, by my own fault, by my most grievous fault," Vincent intoned from an old liturgy containing the form of the Confession.

"Forgive me also, a sinner," Kevin replied.

"You know the details," Vincent began his confession, "but it is important for me to tell you. I need to get them out. Telling it as true as I can, I attacked and sexually assaulted a nun, a sister at a school attached to the parish where I served. I also mutilated her beauty with a knife in a way that can never be restored, and I doubt that she will ever be able to adjust to the outside world again because of her disfigurement. I didn't realize the power of the urge that possessed me when I assaulted her, but when I look back, it was there, disguised all the time."

Vincent hesitated, touching his forehead as if he were trying to remember.

"Go on," Kevin said.

"Do you remember when we were growing up, when you were matter-of-fact about things, and I was just the opposite? The beauty in almost anything, especially the appearance of purity and innocence in the women of the parishes I served, would often emotionally overpower me? I knew I had to restrain myself, and sought counseling and eventually found myself in group meetings with men like myself with their pig-like eyes—pink and hungry but without a scintilla of guilt. But in the end it was my own inordinate, lustful appetite that I fed on that undid me. The tales of distress I heard from the confessional that were attached to the beautiful ones in my congregation drove me to sin again and again, and over the years I left a trail of wounded souls in my wake as I was moved from parish to parish.

"Then at my last parish I met this nun, Sister Mary Celeste, who was so beautiful and innocent that I was almost brought to tears just by the sight of her. No young woman should be so perfect in so many ways. And I was constantly exposed to her—even in the confessional where she confessed to silly things like not saying the Rosary enough—to the extent that her presence soon became too much to endure, and after fighting the urge for so long I finally succumbed to the temptation, and took her in my hands and did it. I possessed and destroyed the beauty I loved, but still couldn't bring myself to feel guilty about it. So here I am and this is my confession."

Kevin Gower had become increasingly restless. He shifted his position and bent toward his brother. "Vincent, Vincent, I am sorely grieved by what I have heard, but will counsel you as best I can before I grant absolution.

"Do not lose hope. That is a sin in itself. First there may be a simple medical solution to your problem, or something else, but as long as you have these obsessive, destructive passions, you must be careful not to expose yourself to the temptations of the flesh. Whatever course your problem takes, know that I will be at your side. First, we must have you evaluated. The Bishop, the Ancient One, who sent you here, has referred you to an old friend of many years in Dublin who has unusual behavioral skills. He is expecting you and will take over your recovery from here.

"Although it may be difficult to adhere to, your penance is simple: Stay away from our mother. As you may have heard, she has for some years been practicing the pagan beliefs of Druidism.

If you are captured by those beliefs, you are doomed. Pray instead to the Holy Mother for consolation and compassion. Let the Church be your place of healing and rehabilitation."

Kevin stood and raised his hand and pronounced the absolution. When he had finished, he said: "The Lord has put away all your sins,"

"Thanks be to God," Vincent said.

As he tossed and turned that night before sleep captured him, Vincent's thoughts were consumed by what little he knew about Druids. He recalled they lived in the pre-Christian era and were supposed to have supernatural abilities. Were there really modern day people who were descended from Druids and had special powers?

DEMONS REIGN

"I'm Father Prescott Ambrose," said the short man in the cassock who opened the door. "You must be Vincent. I've been expecting you."

Vincent stood, frozen in place, capturing the scene. The man standing in front of him was smiling and extending a hand with small, stubby fingers. His head was elongated and terminated in a pinched, baby-like mouth with crooked teeth. The shape of the body filling out the cassock was that of a barrel-shaped trunk attached to short, stubby, extremely bowed legs. The composite image standing before him reminded Vincent of seeing his own distorted shape in a house of mirrors.

"Try not to be alarmed by what you see," Father Prescott said. "Enter and I'll tell you about this place and myself."

When he stepped through the door, Vincent knew immediately he was in the narthex of a church by the smell of incense and the presence of icons. Prescott led him to a door that opened onto a small room that was obviously an office.

"My friends call me Scott," Prescott said. "My enemies, and I have a few, call me something I choose not to repeat. You may call me whatever you wish. Have a seat and please join me in a cocktail. It's that time of day, I believe." He pressed a button and chimes rang throughout the church. Not a minute had passed before a huge man, also in a cassock, with the top of his head shaved into a tonsure entered. He immediately went to a cabinet and opened it to reveal a well stocked bar.

"I have anything you might want," Prescott said, but first let me introduce you to Titus, a Benedictine monk and my assistant. Vincent and Titus nodded to each other, and after the drinks were served, Titus suddenly vanished as if he had been an imaginary presence. Prescott and Vincent turned to face each other.

Prescott unbuttoned his cassock to reveal his legs. They were severely bowed and showed scar evidence of operations to repair breaks.

"I have a rare genetic disorder with a long name—pycnodys-ostosis—better known as Toulouse-Lautrec syndrome, named after the French painter who suffered from the disease. It causes what you see—short stature, deformed and brittle legs, and a lot of other physical abnormalities. You get the picture. As a result I did not function well in the outside world, and found my way to the Church, which discovered I had certain unique talents it could use. My ability to drive out demons was one of them, and so I became an exorcist in a land of magical and mystical happenings. Of course I am also a priest in charge of a parish with a design that seems to forebode evil, and because of that fact, have few parishioners remaining.

"A word about Titus. He was a renowned physician with a practice in Paris, and a bon vivant, I understand. One day, as he tells it, he awoke to a light so intense, that he immediately was made blind, and lost most of the strength in his arms and legs so that he was barely mobile. Over the next few years his handicaps continued and he lost his practice and all of his possessions. Then his friends deserted him. In despair by this point, Titus thought about taking his life. Finally his health failed completely, and he ended up in a hospital where doctors could not diagnose or treat the cause of his malady. His misery was so complete he began to pray, and shouted out continuously for Jesus to heal him. Whenever the doctors or nurses came to his room they would usually find him with his hands raised in supplication, begging Jesus to come into his life. One stormy day, without any warning, there was complete silence in his room. The nurses rushed in to find him sitting in a chair reading the Bible. They were all astonished. How could a man who was at death's door recover so fast? Titus smiled sweetly. He told them he had a vision of the Holy Mother Mary holding the Christ Child, and he fell on his knees and worshipped him; and immediately his eyes were opened and his strength returned. In the process of redeeming himself, Titus took holy orders and eventually ended up here where he has been an invaluable asset."

Prescott put down the glass and focused his full attention on Vincent.

"You, Vincent, have been sent to me to be evaluated; to see what help, if any, the Church can bring to your aid. Perhaps there is a medical diagnosis we can uncover that will offer a cure for your obsessive and violent sexual urges. There is chemical castration, of course, an unpleasant solution; and psychotherapy could also be of help. Then, there is the choice of an exorcism to drive out the demon or demons within who might have taken possession of your passions. All of these are for one purpose: to restore you to your real self and hopefully to service for the Church."

Vincent was caught off base, unaware that exorcism might be a solution. If he was indeed possessed, what else might the demons take of his identity when they departed? He was conflicted and afraid.

"I don't want to be stripped of my personality," he said in a voice suddenly filled with anxiety.

"You won't," Prescott replied. "Your fine Irish humor and spirit would remain. Only your violent carnal quest for the flesh would be removed, and you would become what you started out to be when you took your vows—a dedicated servant of Christ. But again, we do not know if an exorcism is the answer to your problem. As I said, you are here just to be evaluated, and we will start on that tomorrow."

That evening when Vincent went to the small room prepared

for him, he fretted. After tasting all that the flesh had to offer and wanting more, could he ever return to his old way of life in the arms of the Church?

THE DUNGEON

Titus unlocked a heavy door constructed of solid oak. As it opened, it groaned as if it were alive. "Please come in," he said to Vincent.

As Vincent entered, the smells of the room attacked his nostrils: damp, stale, rank air clung to him. It was the smell of a dungeon.

"It was a bomb shelter during the war, Father Gower," Titus explained. "I'm afraid the ventilation system needs some repairs."

The room was not large but seemed that way as it had been stripped of all furniture except for a small bed bolted to the floor and a large chair with restraining straps in the middle of the room, which was bolted down as well. Prescott Ambrose stood at its side. He was dressed in a surplice with a purple stole as was Titus. It was the prescribed dress of an Exorcist. They had been waiting for Vincent Gower to arrive.

Prescott had been certain the physical exam and blood work

would turn up the cause of Vincent's problem, but all the tests had fallen within normal limits. Had he missed something? What was going on? As he thought about it, he decided a reaction that had occurred during the psychotherapy sessions pointed to the answer. The session had started with Vincent seeming to cooperate, but then things took an unpleasant turn as he lay on the couch with Prescott sitting in a chair at his head. Vincent was to respond to Prescott's gentle probing by letting his thoughts play out in free association. It became apparent early on that Vincent was becoming increasingly uncomfortable with the process. He became withdrawn and uncooperative often erupting into angry outbursts when Prescott would insist that he make an effort to participate in the therapeutic process.

The breaking point for Prescott was when Vincent sat up, face red with anger, and began flinging obscenities and threats at him in an unnatural screeching voice. The threats contained foreign words that Prescott did not recognize and he was also certain Vincent couldn't know the words from either his time in seminary or limited travel.

"Who are you to question me, you deformed bastard? It is you who will die on the cross." The unholy voice was emitted with spittle, and Vincent's eyes had become almost translucent.

"Dear Vincent, there is no reason for your truculence," Prescott had responded with a tremor in his voice. He knew he was in the presence of evil. That old serpent, the devil, was in the room.

"I have your complete record from your early days in our own orphanage to the present. In spite of your successes, your file is strewn with loss of control and sexual encounters with women in our parishes, many bordering on rape, most of which have been covered up. But this violent rape and disfigurement of Sister Mary Celeste cannot be excused or glossed over, and your future service to the Church is in doubt. If it were not for the Ancient One, and his considerable influence at the Vatican, you would not be here in my care but in a prison with a long sentence to serve. I am obligated to help you if I can, and since everything else has failed in the past, including intensive psychotherapy, I have decided to try an exorcism. Only the Ancient One is aware of the situation, so instead of being hostile towards me, I would think you would gladly accept this gift for a second chance."

His face still red and twitching but without words, Vincent reluctantly nodded his consent.

Titus led Vincent to the chair and stood beside it as Vincent seated himself and placed his arms over the straps.

"I am sorry, Vincent," Prescott said, "but I must ask you to let us secure the straps around your wrists. Whenever there has been violence from someone who is sitting for the rite of exorcism, the Vatican requires that we restrict that person from rising."

Vincent frowned and looked at Prescott and Titus before submitting to the straps.

"Then it still your wish that the exorcism proceed?" Prescott asked. Once more, Vincent nodded.

Prescott sprinkled Holy Water on himself, Titus and Vincent, laid his hands on Vincent, and made the sign of the cross on him, and then on Titus and himself. Finally, he touched Vincent with a holy relic associated with the Shroud of Turin and began the rite with a series of prayers but excluding the extended Litany of the Saints.

The exorcism began with a plea from Prescott imploring God to free Vincent from the devil that had invaded him. "God, whose nature is ever merciful and forgiving, accept our prayer that this servant of yours, bound by the fetters of sin, may be pardoned by your loving kindness; and pardon the sins of your unworthy servant, that armed with the power of your holy strength, I can attack this cruel, evil spirit in confidence and security."

The moment came for Prescott to confront the demon. "I adjure you, ancient serpent, to depart forthwith in fear along with your savage minions from this servant of God. Do not think of despising my command because you know me to be a great sinner. It is God himself who commands you, the mystic Christ who commands you, God the Holy Spirit who commands you."

Prescott sprinkled Vincent with holy water, and made the sign of the cross on him, and then he and Titus crossed themselves. Prescott pressed the relic against Vincent's body. "I cast you out, unclean spirit, along with every satanic power of the enemy, every specter from hell and all your fell companions, in the name of our Lord Jesus Christ.

"Depart then, impious one, accursed one. Depart with all your deceits, for God has willed that man should be his temple." Vincent began to groan and strain against his restraints. Prescott confronted him again, now with his stole pressed to his forehead.

"Be gone now, be gone seducer . . ."

A loud alarm rang in the room. Prescott immediately stopped the prayer. Titus ran to the wall and hit a switch. An excited voice came over the intercom: "Police are in the Narthex and say they have surrounded the church. They're looking for Father Vincent."

Prescott turned to Vincent. "They must not find you here or we're all doomed. There is a way out."

Titus motioned Vincent to a panel in the wall beside a light switch. When he switched it on, a section of the flooring opened. "Escape route built during the war. Follow it until it ends. Go quickly. You do remember where you're going?"

Vincent nodded and descended the ladder to find he was in a tunnel built as a drain for the property surrounding the church. Water flowed through it carrying debris and dead rats. It had irregular contours, and the water with its current of filth sometimes came up to his knees. On and on he trudged until he came to a ladder that led to an iron cover. It was rusted and hard to move. When he finally opened it, he found he was in an alleyway, which led to a street. Traffic passed by, and it had begun to rain. Vincent had to get away. He turned into the street and began to move with a group of people until he spotted an unattended bicycle lying on its side near the curb. Vincent walked over to the bicycle and stood beside it. No one seemed to notice. He slowly lifted it up and when he did not hear a voice of protest, moved it into the street and pedaled away.

METAMORPHOSIS

Vincent Gower awoke with a jolt. Like a branding iron forced onto his body, a flesh eating pain tore into him. The woman standing beside the bed placed her hand on his arm. She was an older woman with maternal features, and moved her face next to his as if the gauze that encased his head had affected her hearing.

"I'm going to give you something to help, dear. Dr. Royce has left instructions."

Vincent had faced Dr. Sidney Royce in a modest office in a small building adjacent to a hospital in Dublin. He was a tall man with hawkish features who reminded Vincent of a bird of prey falling upon a rabbit in a field near a church where Vincent had once served. Dr Royce was holding a lighted cigarette between his thumb and forefinger as he began to speak.

"Let me say that your face will be remolded so that even your family members will have to take a double look to recognize you, and of course your fingerprints will be removed. You realize this is the last stop in the escape plan that the Ancient One devised. When you have healed, I will give you funds and documentation that cannot be traced so that you can travel anywhere in the world to make a new starts. I have recommended several places down in Africa where the British still have a strong but private presence, or Argentina where some of the Nazi's fled after the war and are still well concealed. There is secure contact information for both locations, but the final decision must be yours as the Church wants to wash its hands of the matter and put this unfortunate incident to rest.

"I would advise you not to return to the United States where one misstep will land you in jail for life. The nun you were once so enamored with to the extent you were willing to sacrifice everything is in a secure location where she cannot be reached. There will be many temptations along the new path you will take to freedom. The decision to resist them is yours to make, but there will be no further attempts to rescue you. When you leave here, it will be as if you have walked through a door from the past that will be forever closed.

The operation had taken place at the Doctor's farm and residence outside of Dublin. They had driven there in a private ambulance to avoid roadblocks. When he finally gained the courage to view himself in a mirror and look at what the acid and skin grafts had done to his face and fingertips, Vincent knew he had gained a new beginning. But what would he do with his remaining time in Ireland?

There was one thing he knew for certain. He had to see his Mother one last time before he left never to return again.

THE DRUID CONNECTION

I t seemed like an entire lifetime since Vincent had visited what he once briefly knew as home, and it almost was. In the vault of his memory, all that was left was vagueness.

A few miles up the coast from Dublin is the coastal town of Drogheda. A few miles to its west, near a bend in the river Boyne, is the megalithic passage tomb of Newgrange. It is the most famous of the five tombs that also include Knowth, Dowth, Fourknocks, Loughcrew, and Tara. Newgrange was built in the mists of pre-Christian history around 3200 BCE. It is said these burial grounds are where the spirits of the deceased of Neolithic communities passed into what they believed was the Otherworld.

These were frightening objects to Vincent as a small child when he visited them with his mother, and was told they were likely built as temples and said to be places of astrological, spiritual, or ceremonial importance to the inhabitants of that age. Now, Vincent would pass Newgrange once more as he journeyed to his mother's small cottage which rested within view of a site known as the Hill of Tara—Tara, from which the high kings of Ireland had ruled and dispensed justice along with their advisors, the powerful Druids.

Druid—after all this time, the word still struck fear in him. Very little was actually known about the Druids, Vincent remembered. They left no written records as their secrets and rituals were passed on by word of mouth and learned by rote. They were the pagan priestly class who had journeyed from the East, he thought, said to be sorcerers who performed human sacrifices and believed in reincarnation.

Julius Caesar, who conquered France in 52 BCE, wrote in his account of the Gallic Wars that Druids were responsible for organizing worship and sacrifices, divination, and judicial procedure in Gaulish, British, and Irish societies. Other writers claimed Druids were held in such respect that if they intervened between two armies they could stop the battle. Still others wrote that their secret rituals were held in groves of oak and mistletoe.

Enough about the Druids, Vincent thought, pulling himself back to the present. He had to focus on reaching his mother's home. His reference point was another hill fort location known as Rath Maeve, according to folklore the dwelling place of the legendary Maeve, the spear-toting, boisterous, and lustful queen who rode defiantly through Celtic sagas.

The region around Newgrange did not resemble the area he had known as a child. Following the directions of villagers along the way, Vincent was able to find the location where his mother lived. The small wood-framed cottage stood at the end of an unpaved path cut into a forest of oak trees. A flickering light could be seen through the windowpanes. Over the stout oaken door rested a recently cut piece of mistletoe. Vincent rapped on the door.

After what seemed an endless moment, a hushed voice came from within, "Who is it at this hour of the day?"

"Mother, it is I, Vincent," he said simply.

A tall woman whose thin face was partially hidden by an abundance of grey hair opened the door. She stood without moving, framed by the yellow light emanating from the room. She looked neither old nor young but simply as if she were part of the surroundings. She raised a gnarled, arthritic hand to shade her eyes as she peered at him in the fading light of the day.

Danu took a second look, and then cried out as she fell into his arms, "Vincent, Vincent, is it really you?"

She was named Danu after the mother of an important family of the gods, the Tuatha De Dannan. According to Irish folklore, they were descended from a race of people skilled in the arts of druidism and magic that came to Ireland from afar long before recorded history and now lived in the Otherworld, a place accessible only through lakes and passage graves like Newgrange.

Danu's husband, Liam, had been shot as a traitor in one of the continuing Irish wars of independence, and she had been left with the care of Vincent and his brothers. Only Liam's dearest and closest friend, later to become a bishop and serve in the Vatican, would secretly support her. After refusing to recant her druid beliefs when being accused of being an unfit mother, Danu's children were taken from her and placed in a home for orphans. Danu never recanted, and retired to the oak- and mistletoe-forested area near the great passage graves, the center for the few remaining druid rituals in Ireland.

Danu led Vincent into a small visiting room adjoining the kitchen. "What brings you here after so many years, my son?" she asked.

"It is a long and uncomfortable story, mother, but one you need to hear," he said, and leaned back in his chair and began to speak in a remote, dream-like voice. When Vincent told Danu what had finally brought him back to Ireland, and what his brother Kevin and all the others had suggested, she placed her head in her hands and moaned. After what seemed like an interminable moment, she turned to her son.

"Vincent, do you remember the story about Lucet Mael, perhaps the greatest of all druids?"

"I've heard of him but don't remember all the details."

"Well, here is the story as it has been told: Loegaire, head of the mightiest of Irish families and King of Tara, was troubled. News of a stranger traveling from region to region spreading a new and false religion had reached him. Wanting to know more, he turned to the man he trusted most, the druid Lucet Mael, and asked him to perform the ritual known as the Imbas Forosna, 'the knowledge that enlightens.'

"Taking a piece of raw dog flesh from a pouch, Lucet Mael chewed it for a few moments and placed it on a stone in his dwelling. The druid prayed over the meat and asked the gods to help him foretell the future. He then lay down with his hands pressed against his cheeks and awaited the sleep that would transport him to the Otherworld.

"When he awoke, Lucet Mael trembled from the knowledge that had been revealed to him. A teaching from across the seas had been brought into the land that would overcome all who resisted it. The teaching was that of Christianity and its bearer was the man known as St. Patrick."

"What does that have to do with me?" Vincent asked.

"The answers to all your questions about yourself and your inner healing rest in the ritual," Danu said. "You must perform the Imbas Forosna yourself, and once you reach the Otherworld, the gods will tell you all you need to know and guide you on your way."

Danu rose and walked into a small kitchen where an ancient refrigerator shook and groaned as if to announce her arrival. When she returned to Vincent she had a small pouch in her hand. "Here is the raw meat for you to begin your journey," she said.

JOURNEY TO THE OTHERWORLD

D anu led Vincent into a small room with a single bed frame positioned in the center that held a mattress directly on wooden slats. A large stone that served as a stand was positioned at the head of the bed.

"Remember the steps you must perform. They must be done precisely or the journey will not take place," she said. Danu kissed her son and backed out of the room. Vincent opened the pouch and looked at the piece of raw meat. It was dark colored and coarse, and when he drew it towards his nose, emitted the smell of a wild animal. He hesitated briefly, but remembering his mother's admonition placed the piece of meat in his mouth and began to chew. A gamey taste soured his mouth, but he continued to chew until the meat became as malleable as a piece of gum. Then he placed it on the stone beside the bed and prayed to whatever gods were present that he would be successful in performing the druid ritual, the Imbas Forosna, the knowledge that enlightens, which would reveal the course of future events.

Vincent then lay down on the bed with his hands resting on his cheeks, closed his eyes, and awaited the sleep he hoped would transport him to the Otherworld. Somewhere near the Hill of Tara there was a loud clap of thunder.

In his dream, Vincent found himself facing a long tunnel covered by ivy. At the end, beckoning him, was a man of enormous size with a white beard and dressed in a roughly woven woolen cloak girded at the waist. In his right hand he carried a wand. At his feet rested a large egg resembling the texture and color of the mineral serpentine. Vincent continued down the long tunnel until he stood before what he now realized must be the ancient figure of a Celtic god.

"I have no name for you to call me," the figure said. "I am the leader of the Tuatha De Danaan, the Celtic gods you now wish to call upon. You must come no further. Look at my feet and you will see a magic egg made from the hissing of angry serpents. It protects the gods against evil incantations and intentions from unbelievers. For you to ponder, your fate is already written in the blood of many sacrifices that have gone before you. Like them, you will be despised and pursued. Lo, before you is a vision from the future, but do not worry for the souls of men are immortal, and after a fixed number of years according to their bravery they enter another body. So will yours if you only believe and obey. Now return from whence you came, and your dreams from the Imbas Forosna will tell you of those things which you can change in your life and all that is fixed by fate."

Vincent started to awaken. The meat he had chewed still rested on the stone table. The taste remained acrid in his mouth. As consciousness continued to return, Vincent began to writhe in his bed like a snake on a piece of marble. His arms flailed and his legs jerked uncontrollably.

When he could finally get out of bed, he careened like a drunken man around the bedroom until he found a door, which he

flung open. In the small room before him he found his mother reading.

Vincent's face was a mask of horror. "Mother, mother," he
screamed. "I have been shown the gates of Hell." Danu dropped
her book and ran to him.

"Tell me, tell me!" she exclaimed.

"I had a vision," Vincent said, and clutched his mother.
"There was an ancient figure, a leader of the Celtic gods, who revealed to me a tall wooden structure resembling a man, and the man
had been set on fire and there were people inside who were screaming
and trying to escape. As I stood there, the structure collapsed in a
fiery heap, and I could still see people inside. In the dream, I was
one of them. It was horrible. Mother, you know about these things.
What does it mean?"

Danu raised her eyes as if she were looking to heaven. There
was a flicker of teeth, and saliva on her lips when she spoke. "Our
druid brothers left no written history. All of what we know comes
from the ancients and from the mists of time itself. We believe that
our souls live on forever and after a time find another form. There-
fore, you must not fear death. I urge you to continue your use of
the Imbas Forosna to foretell your fate in this existence and prepare
you for the next. All of our destinies are written in the stars, and we
must have the courage to live into them. Now go and rest. We must
leave shortly. I will take you to a place where you will be safe."

Danu left the house and when she returned, she arrived with
a large man with broad shoulders whose pants were supported by
suspenders. One strap was twisted and his shirttail hung out.

"Woke me up, she did," was all he said.

An ancient car stood beside the road that led to Danu's
house. Vincent had dozed off. She gently shook him awake.

"We must leave now. Quickly gather your things!"

For what seemed like hours, the rumpled man Danu called Tim drove
them through the night to a remote village that was rumored to be
one of the few remaining centers of Druid lore and activity. Most
of the homes had been built to form a large circle. In the center was
a fire pit of sorts with burnt timbers and a partially built structure
which, when finished, would look something like a man. Vincent

remembered the vision of the burning man-like figure from his dream that had terrified him. There were no churches in the village. Tim stopped before a nondescript house set back from the circle in a second row.

"Tim's sister and granddaughter live here," Dana said. "Tim called ahead. They're expecting us."

A young woman with a face that seemed pinched together answered the door.

"Hello. I'm Maeve. Named after the wicked Queen, I'm afraid. Please come in."

Danu and Tim left with admonitions for Vincent to remain in the village now known as Camus until he received instructions that the intensive search for him had waned. But it was not to be. Somehow the authorities had broken the secrecy of the escape plan and knew that like a pursued animal, Vincent had holed up somewhere. He would not be leaving Ireland anytime soon.

It would be on a waning moon, partly revealed by scudding clouds, that Vincent would finally decipher the design of a village encircling a huge fire pit. He arose to the sounds of construction. Men, some whom he had met, were building a form and bending strips of wicker over it. As he watched, he realized that the construction was taking the shape of a man with arms and legs and a papier-mâché head ready to be placed on top. Vincent remembered his dream. He was looking at a wicker figure of a man who was to be set on fire. Then he realized its significance. It was the beginning of May when a sacrifice was made for the success of the crops. The stick-man figure was ready to be burned.

It was evening when the sacrificial burning was performed. Vincent and Maeve had arrived. A maypole had been erected and dancers had assembled to the sound of music. Even with the chill of the evening, she and other women from the village had removed their blouses and grasped a ribbon to begin the movement around the pole. Like molting insects, many of the men had shed most of their garments. All were dancing with abandon. Vincent was not surprised. With a sly, promising smile, Maeve had told him what would happen.

The wicker figure was ready to collapse in a shower of fiery embers when the police arrived to raid the ceremony. Dancers were caught unawares as sirens shrieked and vehicles entered the village. Nude figures clutched their clothes and ran. Many were stopped and questioned. Wanted notices with photos were distributed. Where was the notorious Vincent Gower?

Far from the madness in the square where villagers were cornered and the wicker figure smoldered, Maeve led Vincent to a small house maintained by an ancient looking, grey-haired widow who surprised Vincent as she shed her wig. She escorted him to a concealed trap door that disclosed a staircase, which led to a furnished basement beneath the cottage.

PART II

HOLY MOUNTAIN

THE CONVENT

In time I was reassigned and arrived with meager luggage in hand at a new convent. I must say Our Lady of Perpetual Help was located in a strange place on top of a remote part of a mountain in Tennessee. It was only by a process of attrition, elimination, and forbearance that one day I was to become Mother Superior Mary Celeste.

I can painfully recall the period of my life before I came to "The Mountain," as it was called. The knowledge that the body I had dedicated to God had been violated and maimed dragged me into a pit of depression so black I could not function, and I was soon removed from my position as a teacher at our convent's school. My family's pain was evident. Even with their assurances, I could hardly face them when it became apparent that I was pregnant. The months that followed were as if I was caught in a nightmare that never ended. Press coverage was intense. I was hounded, pursued really, almost as if I were a movie star.

The diocese was having a difficult time with the distractions that only seemed to increase as long as Father Vincent was missing. Was he close at hand, waiting for the right moment to strike again? The police provided security, but this only increased the interest. I was transferred from my parish to the diocesan office where the Bishop and his staff attempted to handle the never dying curiosity of the news media.

One day, after my pregnancy had reached six months, I was sent away to a shelter of sorts for unwed mothers located in Baltimore, Maryland. The irony of the situation was not lost on me! The shelter turned out to be a large brick building in a poverty-stricken section of the city. Most of the girls were from that part of town, and I fast became a curiosity. Were there really women who took vows not to 'do it' and prayed most of the time? I believe I did some good while I was there. They found I was a normal person with the exception of my 'weird-o' ideas, and we actually had some good discussions about the Virgin Mary who also experienced the pain that was about to happen to each of us. As we came closer to the time when our water would break, we were placed in a room together, and when mine broke, they helped me from the bed and together kept saying, "It's going to be all right. We're here for you." When I had come to term, I was told the Church would handle all the details of the birth, and the child would be adopted by a "deserving Catholic family." I thought I would get to see and hold my baby, but it was taken from my body by caesarian section, and it was only later that I was told it was a girl.

The shock of everything that happened was so great, I eventually ended up in what they called a "rest home," and when I didn't improve enough to function as the Church wanted and needed, I was sent to a place so secret, its name and location was omitted from any list of convents.

The sisters and I occupy the whole of a mansion designed to look like a castle, which is perched on the precipice of the highest reach of the mountain. An eccentric English couple had built the imposing structure in 1861 complete with ramparts, spires, and a moat, all of the stone quarried from the mountain itself. Upon their death, the property had languished until the Catholic Church purchased it for the site of a convent for nuns who had lost their way in their dedication to the faith.

That was one way of putting it, but the truth was that the nuns were all disturbed sisters; their wills had not yet been remolded so they could serve the Church as brides of Christ. Most had run away from other convents, but could not handle the outside world and had crawled back sniffling when their own families could not accept the disgrace of a fallen nun.

Some tried again and again to escape and ended up on the street until the "Church" came and "rescued" them and sent them to this place which had been chosen so they couldn't escape—one sealed off from the outside world except for a small college nearby that was virtually impossible to reach on foot because of the terrain. Besides, all the doors to Our Lady, as we called it, remained locked except for the one leading to the garden, and the nuns working there were monitored. You can imagine from this scenario that as Mother Superior I had to be tough, and tough you might guess, was still not part of my nature at the time.

Our Lady of Perpetual Help had a huge cross that stood fifty feet high on a precipice shining its healing grace into the valley beneath. Yet there was little contact with the inhabitants there. We in the convent were devoted solely to prayer, reflection, confession, and an occasional retreat, growing a garden for our vegetables, and supporting ourselves by making delicately scented soaps, which were treasured by expensive boutiques in many parts of the country.

So it happened that after many years I began to put the events of the past behind, and I was slowly able to relax and begin to live into the present moment. However, the memory of my lost child had found a protected place within my heart where I could go and be with her through the years as she grew. I remember often thinking through the long years of separation that she must be beginning Kindergarten or learning to drive a car or now is about the time she'd be graduating from high school. I wondered if she went to college or if she had a boyfriend or had married young. Regardless, every time I thought of her, I smiled inwardly, and reveled in the fact that my child was growing up.

MIRROR, MIRROR, ON THE WALL

Most of the nuns called me Mary Celeste to my back. It was as if the lack of an ear had impaired my hearing. It was only when they faced me that they added the "Mother."

It was all right. Most of them remembered what kind of emotional shape I was in when I first passed through Our Lady's doors. But over the years I had changed and most of them hadn't. At least, that's what I thought. I was now the more assertive and self-assured nun, the one that had finally "pulled it all together."

And then one day I let my guard down and did something that violated the commitment I had made to be in the world but not of the world. Vanity and something else had gotten hold of me.

In the bowels of the convent-castle we occupied, I had discovered a gold-tinted and burnished, high backed chair, which I fancied, and had it brought to my office. The sisters jokingly called the chair my "gilded throne" for that is where I sat when I talked with them about personal matters or where I met people from outside Our Lady.

I was sometimes accompanied on my "throne" by a mongrel dog that showed up at our gate so sick it could hardly stand. In a mountainous terrain where deerhounds reign supreme, this scrawny, black cur stood no chance at survival except for the grace of the one who rules over everything. I never had any exposure to dogs growing up, but the dog took to me, and my guests would often find him sitting beside me staring out at them with his black inscrutable eyes.

One indescribable day, driven by an urge I cannot explain or define, I stood before my gilded throne and took off all my clothing—not a piece of my habit or underclothing remained. I was completely nude. At the rear of a closet, turned so that it faced the wall, was a mirror five feet tall. It was framed with cheap plastic and backed with cardboard. In a moment of vanity I had purchased it on an outing to try to picture in my mind how I once looked. Yet, I was afraid to use it, and so that I wouldn't be tempted to do so, I turned it to face the wall.

I removed the mirror from the closet and hung it on the wall. It was covered with dust and I got a cloth and cleaned it. "What a pitiful sight," I thought. Whenever I was clothed in my habit, my clothing reflected the importance of my position. Now I was just another naked, disfigured woman.

I examined myself more intensely in the mirror. My hair which had once been described as the color of honey with a hint of strawberry was turning into a dingy orange color shot through with streaks of grey; my smooth, lightly freckled pale skin now the color of dollar store chalk. As I looked downward from where my left ear had been severed, I saw a long jagged scar that was once red but now white with age. It ran down my neck to my collarbone before skipping like a shell skimming the water leaving little splashes wherever it touched until it arrived at my left breast where a cruel cut had removed both my areola and nipple.

Finally I saw on the no longer so taut skin of my lower abdomen the wicked scar that Vincent Gower had not made, it was the scar left by the caesarian section when I had come to term. It seems a priest arrived and had prevented the doctors from cleaning out the semen. When I look back on it now, I know there was a special purpose to the priest's intervention, one of which I was not then aware.

As I prepared to put the mirror back in the closet and turn its glass to the wall, I looked at my ravaged scarecrow body one last time. I would cover it with my Habit and once more adopt the mask of the soul-wounded victims of this world's madness. I prayed my child would not become one of them.

PART THREE

GROUNDWORK

THE HOLLOW

"Hello, Ma'am. I'm Victor Gant," Vincent Gower said. "Read your help wanted note on the bulletin board down at the farmers' market."

The woman facing him had the look of fatigue and frustration etched on her face. She had her hand on her hip. "I'm looking for someone to help me here," she said. "My husband died a short time ago, and I can't do it myself with part-time help."

Her name was Maggie Bullock. She was a raw-boned mountain woman in her mid-forties with once red hair shading towards auburn. Her face and arms were covered with freckles. "Like I said," she continued, as if it were a subject she couldn't stop talking about, "My man's been dead a year now. Was a lineman for the county. Got caught up in the big storm that hit the mountain last year."

Maggie stepped out on the porch until she could look up at the mountain and pointed. "See that big cross they built up there? Behind it is a convent. Nuns, you know. Strange story behind it, but anyway, that's where it happened. The whole mountain was blacked out. Billy was up there helping the electric people get the power back on, and a tree fell down across the lines and that's how he got kilt."

Vincent put on a pained look at the revelation, but he already knew what the cross, and the strange looking convent called Our Lady of Perpetual Help, looked like, and what was behind its doors.

With his escape network uncovered and wrapped up, his mother threatened, and his documents suspect, Vincent had used what funds remained to buy both his and Maeve's way into the United States where he settled for work harvesting crops in south Florida. Maeve took jobs working as a maid in second-rate motels along US Highway 1 where the owners barely glanced at her forged credentials. Vincent would come in tired and dirty from the fields, and her fatigue from long hours spent at menial work caused her face to continue to contract as if it had been tightened in a vise.

"We can't keep on living this way," Maeve finally said to Vincent one evening as they were sitting on the edge of a mattress with sagging springs. "It's taking its toll on both of us. Suppose this prophecy that haunts you isn't true. Suppose the nun you need to find is dead. Can't we just move on with our lives and settle somewhere."

That somewhere turned out to be Tennessee. Vincent had been blessed with two revelations: one was that farmers in a rich agricultural area along the Cumberland Plateau were expecting a bumper crop and advertising top pay for hardworking farm hands. The other came from a Catholic television program. Vincent saw a Mass being held at a convent located on a remote mountain in Tennessee. On the front row near the altar sat the Mother Superior, and behind her a group of nuns fingering their rosaries. Vincent did a double take. Age had taken its toll on her once perfect features, but he would recognize Mary Celeste anywhere. Vincent and Maeve packed up their ancient Volkswagen and headed for Tennessee.

With their arrival in the valley below the small town of Sewanee, Vincent was ready for the next step in the plan slowly taking shape in his mind. He purchased a topographical map of the mountains that brooded over the plateau, and pinpointed the area where the college and convent were located. Then he visited the County Courthouse and went straight to the Property/Taxes Department where he found the exact information he was seeking. There were several access points along the route up the mountain that he could take to reach the convent, but when he found the posted notice for help, the decision was made for him—his first stop would be to visit the Bullock's property. Like a writer slowly developing a plot and narrative, he was one step closer to piecing all the parts together in a grand plan that now seized his mind. The first part was: Building a Druid fortress in the midst of a rural community in Tennessee.

The other was out of his control. As in the symbiotic pull of opposites, he was drawn toward the presence of Mary Celeste like a moth toward a flame. As much as he fought the desire, the essence of her had never left his senses. Now that he was so near, he had to see the isolated convent where she was confined, and where in his fantasy he would rescue her. The trip took him up a steep mountain incline to a place where the road leveled off. From there he entered the domain of a small college and beyond it, the gravel road that led to the convent. As Vincent approached the strange looking structure, he found himself blocked by a tall fence with a sturdy gate and callbox, but he had a clear view of what lay beyond. Our Lady of Perpetual Help rested on the precipice directly above the widow Bullock's property. Vincent caught his breath. He was so close but yet so far.

Vincent shifted his gaze away from the cross above, and bent closer to Maggie Bullock until he was able to lock his eyes on hers, then he arranged his face in that sincere look that had always impressed the nuns in the many churches where he had once been assigned. "Ma'am, I been working on the farms further down the valley from dawn to dusk so I know what hard work is. Just tell me what you need done."

For a few seconds Maggie was frozen in place by the fixated look on Vincent's face. Finally she broke his stare and stepped back to take a better look. She had plenty of experience with men when she was younger, and could tell he once had been a handsome specimen of a man, and still was in a strange sort of way. His tanned skin was smooth but as thin as parchment drawn tight over prominent facial bones. Too tight and too smooth, she thought, almost as if he had been made up for a stage role. He had green eyes that were sexy and scary at the same time the way they bored into you as if they were peering into your soul. No softness there, she thought, but one of possession with perhaps a hint of cruelty mixed in. For a moment Maggie hesitated in making a decision, but when she looked at the whole man, she could see his body was hard from the kind of backbreaking work she knew only too well. She knew he could do the work.

"To the right is what's left of the corn field," she said. "Needs to be plowed under for spring planting. We got hay out there still lying on the ground, and there's a bunch of other stuff that needs to be done. I'll have to make you a list. I know you're not from around here, and I don't want nobody that's going to be coming and going, so if you work for me you got to live close by. If this works for you, there's an old hunting shack down in the hollow back there. Boys used it to camp and hunt. Then they growed up and left, and now Billy's dead. It ain't much, but there's a well for water, and plenty of firewood. Better than having to drive back and forth, and you can stay there free if you keep it up."

The more Vincent looked at Maggie, and the opportunity that had just fallen into his hands, the more incredible it seemed. Something he had only dreamed of—a place where he and his followers could live. Where he would be the sole ruler. A place right under the noses of the authorities in a small valley near the convent where the woman resided whose capture and possession would finally set him free from the torment he had endured all these years.

Vincent prepared to descend into a secluded vale like one he had only read about and visited in his dreams—a place the ancients described as a sacred place where Druids gathered and sometimes lived. Vincent approached it with a gnawing sense of trepidation. The holy of holies lay before him. He trembled as he stepped to the edge to enter. He took Maeve by the hand.

The descent led down a series of steps cut into mountain sandstone. Once down, an expanse below opened up into a setting of unimaginable beauty. Before him, in absolute solitude, was a pristine vista of moss-covered oaks, and a stream bordered by willows ran through it. Colorful birds rested on the boughs of the trees, and the fleeting images of deer retreating further into the woods were only a minor disruption to the serenity of the scene.

As Vincent and Maeve ventured further, the Hollow began to flatten out and they could see the terrain change as it rose to meet the mountain. But nothing they saw erased the beauty of the Hollow itself.

All that Vincent saw was his for the taking, and he knew how to do it. But where was he going to find the labor to transform the Hollow into his Druid haven? That night, as Vincent spent his first night in the Hollow, resting in a sleeping bag next to Maeve, and looking up at the panoply of stars in the heavens, he had no answers but knew that somehow it would happen...

SNAKE EYES

"We handle snakes," was all she said. After two weeks of watching Vincent Gower's backbreaking work on the farm, Maggie invited the man she knew as Victor Gant to attend church with her.

With the exception of the stringy haired, wild-eyed girl named Maeve who had linked her life to his, Vincent Gower had no friends or following. Vincent thought about the invitation. If he played it right, going to church was a chance to attract disciples even if they did handle snakes.

Finding the Primitive Pentecostal Church was no easy matter unless you knew the twists and turns of roads that ran between mountain and valley. After a bumpy two-mile ride on a hardpan surface in Maggie's car, Vincent and Maggie arrived at a small parking area.

They walked up a narrow dirt path to a small, white washed, wooden church. There was a glass-framed bulletin board to the right of the entrance. It contained events that were happening that month. At the top was a biblical quotation from the gospel of Mark: "And these signs will accompany those who believe. In my name they shall speak with new tongues. They shall take up serpents, and if they drink any deadly thing, it shall not hurt them."

There was noise coming from within the church. The dying words of the hymn "The Old Rugged Cross" were still echoing when, with a loud squeak from rusty hinges, Maggie slowly opened the door. Inside the church, on wooden benches, sat an assortment of about fifty men, women, and children. The men wore mainly coveralls or denim clothing with short or rolled up sleeves, the women plain button-up dresses and no makeup.

The preacher was thin with straight unruly grey hair, and wore threadbare brown corduroy pants supported by red suspenders. He stood on a dais shaped like a cross that had been placed on the stage at the front of the church. His tongue was wagging from side to side and sounds were coming from his mouth that reminded Vincent of the chatter of a tobacco auctioneer. A man and woman on the front row stood up and began to respond to the preacher in singsong voices. Then they turned to the rest of the congregation.

"They're speaking in tongues," Maggie said to Vincent. "The man and woman are going to interpret what he's saying."

The man was as thin as a reed and had red hair. The woman was just the opposite and was huge below the waist as if the upper part of her had just slipped down like a landslide.

"God's done give us a new snake," the thin man shouted.

"He sure has, and Preacher's got him here," the fat woman said.

Maggie began to whimper and squeezed Vincent's arm. He could feel her nails in his flesh.

The preacher squinted as he looked back at Maggie and the stranger. "Hello, Maggie. See you brought someone with you. Welcome, brother."

The congregation turned to look at Vincent. He felt Maggie's nails dig in deeper.

The preacher smiled. "I'm afraid our 'Sara' you know, 'Seraph', has passed on. Meet our new serpent 'Tim.' Tim-ber Rattler.

Ya'll get it? Found him back in the woods. He's a specimen! Almost five feet long with vicious lookin' curved fangs. Looked it up. Book says they pack a lot of venom. They bite you, you almost always die. Okay Henry, bring ole Tim out."

Henry, the man with the red hair, bounded up the steps of the small stage where the preacher stood and went behind the curtain. After some shuffling backstage, he returned with the cage and opened the door. Inside a snake was hissing.

Maggie remembered the words "tremble, tremble, tremble," from an old Gospel hymn and began to shake.

The preacher squatted and looked into the cage. His arm showed the scars and deformities of numerous snake bites. His hand moved ever closer to the opening. Maggie began to groan and clutched Vincent on the thigh with her other hand. The preacher diverted the snake with a small wooden rod. When the snake struck the rod, the preacher's hand darted inside and grasped the snake holding it behind the head so it couldn't turn to bite him.

"Here's ole Tim," he shouted, pulling the snake out and holding it high above him. The congregation began to clap and the pungent smell of sweat filled the room. The preacher swung the snake from side to side. Then the sound of silence filled all the space in the building.

The preacher smiled and began to speak to the snake when the unthinkable happened. The snake, yellowish brown with black crossbars, and as thick as the heavy part of a baseball bat, swung its massive body. Its tail with the rattles struck the preacher in the right thigh. The blow and the sinister sound of the rattles could be heard to the back row of the small church. When the preacher flinched and loosened his grip, the timber rattler twisted his head and struck. The preacher grasped his left shoulder and cried out. The serpent fell to the hard wood of the dais and began to wiggle and squirm its way across the shape of the cross.

Vincent disengaged his arm from Maggie's death grip, and stood to survey a chaotic scene. Henry, the assistant, rushed to help the preacher who cried out in a loud voice and tried to move, but collapsed in the path of the snake. Women screamed and groaned. Children cried. Men stood up and stared.

Vincent stepped away from the pew, ran down the aisle, and with one arm vaulted onto the stage. He crouched in front of the snake that immediately spiraled into a striking position. Balanced on his haunches, Vincent swiveled his body back and forth in front of the snake like a mongoose preparing to attack a cobra.

Men from the congregation and a few women crowded in front of the stage to watch the contest. Others pulled their children to their sides and wrapped their arms around them. Vincent continued to feint an attack first with his left hand then with his right. Faster and faster he moved his hands. Closer and closer he inched his way towards the snake whose head was trying to follow the movement. Then, quicker than the snake could react, Vincent's right hand shot forth and grasped the snake behind the head. Vincent stood and began to choke "ole Tim." The congregation started to cheer. The serpent thrashed his tail back and forth, his rattles sounding like Congo drums being struck by a madman. When the snake finally went limp, Vincent threw it to the floor and stomped on its head. "The serpent loses," he said in a loud voice to his audience. Without another word he jumped from the stage, took Maggie by the hand and left the church. Most of the congregation streamed outside to watch Vincent and Maggie walk down the gravel path to their car and drive off. As Vincent wheeled the car around, he could hear a loud voice exclaiming, "Who is that man?"

When they reached the door to Maggie's house, Vincent opened the door and followed Maggie inside. She began to tremble and turned to face him.

"Who are you?" she whispered.

Vincent moved to face her and began to remove her clothes. "You're about to find out," he said.

THE MAKING
OF BOGIE

Although it was not quite daylight, Vincent Gower, known by everyone in the camp as Victor Gant, shook himself awake as the sound of workers arriving on the construction site penetrated his consciousness. Bits and pieces of their conversation were slowly becoming recognizable. The deep, husky vocals of the males could be heard directing the flow of activity with the voices of the females adding to the instructions. He smiled and nodded his head in relief. He had been concerned about how he was going to get the wicker-constructed specter resembling a man built in time for the May Day fertility rites with just the help of a few construction workers from the congregation at church. Then something happened that would have seemed like divine intervention if he had believed in an all-powerful deity. Instead, it was just another piece of "Vincent's Luck" added to the puzzle that was taking shape in his mind.

Just when Vincent thought he had hit a wall with the project, he came across an announcement in a local paper about a horror movie coming to a local theater. It told the story of a devout Christian policeman who discovered an evil pagan cult located on a remote island. When he investigated, he was tricked into participating in a fertility rite where he became the sacrifice and was burned alive in a large wicker construction resembling a man. The movie had developed a huge cult following among the young "peace and flower" crowd despite evidence of it being inspired by one of the most brutal ways the ancient Druids performed human sacrifices.

Vincent's luck multiplied when a reporter from a Chattanooga paper received a tip that there was a man in a remote Tennessee valley who was planning to celebrate the vernal equinox and coming of spring to the region by building a giant facsimile of a man named Bogie and conducting a pagan ceremony. The article was picked up by the Associated Press and reprinted by most of the national newspaper chains.

The "pagan ritual" aspect aroused the ire of a fundamentalist Christian community pastor who commented in a letter to the editor: "Who among us is going to show up at something like that?" Someone replied that the preacher hadn't considered that during a ten-year period the country had experienced the Vietnam War, Woodstock, a drug culture, Haight-Ashbury, flower children and a back-to-nature movement.

When young people from those groups began to show up in the valley beneath the Cumberland Plateau, it didn't surprise Vincent. Their arrival wasn't a problem for him at the time, but he knew that with so much attention being focused on the building of a giant wood and straw man, it would just be a matter of time before the press would be all over the story, and he remembered the words from a poem: "But at my back I always hear/Time's wingèd chariot hurrying near," and he knew he couldn't keep his presence a secret much longer.

As Vincent lay listening to the sounds and rhythms of the breaking dawn, he found himself trying to recapture the experience of taking the sacred vows when accepting the ancient faith of Druidism, and participating in the ritual, Imbas Forosna, where he had experienced a vision of the burning of a Wicker Man from pre-Christian history. The burning man frightened him, and the experience was reinforced when he visited the site of an actual human sacrifice. It was there at an historical exhibit that he saw the remaining framework of a burned Wicker Man structure almost identical to the one he was building, and with it the encased ashes of the victims.

Vincent felt the movement of a body pressing against his side. Lying beside him on the bed was his companion Maeve. The early light softened the pinched together aspect of her face. Low moans came from parched lips, and her body began to jerk as she started to awaken.

Vincent frowned. He remembered he had a problem. There was a growing resentment towards Maeve among some of his female followers. She was his earliest disciple and had worked tirelessly by his side. But she had gotten so damn possessive and antagonistic toward the other females that they now stood around waiting for her to show a weakness so like a pack of wolves they could devour her. Vincent's task was to hold all the females in camp, because if they left, many of the men they had drawn into the construction crew would also. He would need them all to make his plan work.

Vincent slipped out of bed, donned his work clothes, and turned on the propane stove to heat up coffee from yesterday. He picked up the roll of drawings he was using for the construction of Bogie, and with a mug in hand headed toward the construction site. No equipment had been available for digging postholes in the remote hollow filled with oak trees so they had to be dug by hand. In the first step of the process, stout oak timbers were embedded in the postholes to resemble legs and concrete poured to hold them in the proper position. Wicker and bamboo from the nearby stream, and hay from the fields, were now being wrapped around the posts to form the body. Atop a platform attached to the posts an enclosure in the shape of a man's trunk with arms and a head was being built. Leading up to the enclosure was a detachable ladder. The entire structure was to measure almost fifty feet in height.

When Vincent arrived at the site, he saw Ed Perry, the man in charge of construction, cautioning the crew to be careful with the final touches on the project and to clean up the site. Vincent thought the females seemed to enjoy the process of building Bogie, called by some the 'Bogeyman', whom they had been threatened with as children. They were all pretty young and looked to be in their late teens or early twenties. Many sported tattoos and piercings, and most had that coarse sandpaper look that comes from an unhealthy diet and bad habits. There would soon be among them one who would immediately catch Vincent's eye. Her healthy looking pale pink skin would display neither tattoos nor piercings. Wide green eyes would wrinkle with apparent pleasure as she turned her body towards him, and he would smile as he ran his eyes over her. The last features that would cause that familiar stirring inside would be the gorgeous outline of her body, and her hair—shining natural soft curls and his favorite hair color—red, neither dark nor light, but the luscious shade of a strawberry nestled in its bed of straw, and to top it all off, she would wear a spray of white dogwood blossoms in her hair.

Vincent would not be able to take his eyes off of her.

THE GIRL WITH THE STRAWBERRY HAIR

The girl with the strawberry hair stood at the top of the depression in the valley floor called the Hollow. People who had seen the Hollow said there was a stream that ran through it flanked on both sides by birch and willow trees, but her immediate impression of the scene was that of oak trees spotted with mistletoe and draped with moss. That's all she knew about the place except there was a man in charge named Victor Gant who was the primary subject of her investigation.

She slipped over the lip of the Hollow onto the steps that led to the bottom. There, where the land flattened out she could see a crowd milling about. They were apparently completing the final work on a clearing with lighting and benches—some kind of recreation area, she thought. To the left of the clearing stood a huge wooden structure resembling a man. She knew from reports this was the structure the man named Victor Gant referred to as Bogie, and intended to burn in a fertility rite.

As the girl with the strawberry hair scanned the crowd, she recognized several of the workers she had seen when she arrived in the small town of Cowan, Tennessee. One was a thin girl named Angie with a bad complexion who was dressed in a gaudy multi-colored skirt. She had run into her in town peddling scarves.

Angie stopped talking with another girl and walked over to greet her. "Hey, Red. See you made it. Come on over and meet the guys, and I'll show you around."

Most of the "guys" were girls. The girl now dubbed 'Red' had dressed down with jeans and a light inexpensive jacket that covered her top. She received only a polite smile from most of the girls.

Angie was preening herself as she announced, "I'm going to show Red around and I'll be back in a few." With an officious flourish she pointed to an area being cleared. "What we're doing here is opening up this space as a meeting place where we can all gather, a place to dance and stuff like that," Angie said and pointed to where the girls were working.

Red's real name was Scarlett O'Quinn. She was named Scarlett by the nurses in the delivery room because of the unusual shade of her red hair. At birth it wasn't really red as in flaming red, but the color of a strawberry nestled in the straw with the sheen of morning dew still on it. By the time she was handed over to the nuns at a nearby Catholic facility, the name Scarlett had stuck, so calling her Mary, Elizabeth, or some other name from the Bible no longer seemed appropriate. After the Church had used its considerable power to hide all evidence of her parentage, she was adopted by the childless O'Quinns of Nashville, Tennessee, whose good fortune it was to be wealthy and in the upper echelons of Nashville's storied, high society.

Scarlett found out in a rather rude way that she was adopted. A little friend who heard it from her mother told her. Scarlett ran up the driveway into the house. What did it mean to be adopted, six-year-old Scarlett asked Frances, her mother.

"Well, honey, it means that the woman who gave birth to you couldn't take care of you, but loved you enough to let you be our daughter."

That answer left the door open for other questions that Frances couldn't answer. Scarlett couldn't forget the look on Frances's face. When Russell, Scarlett's high-powered attorney father didn't give her any more information than "We never met your birth-mother, and the file has been sealed," Scarlett, who was very precocious, thought, "One day I'll open that file and find the woman who gave birth to me."

With her past identity seemingly erased, Scarlett grew up with all the outward trappings and inward virtues expected of Nashville's privileged classes. With her exquisite bodily proportions poured into a pale green gown, and her escort smiling and almost tongue-tied at what he was seeing, she was the most photographed debutante at the Cotillion. Then she was off to college at Vanderbilt followed by law school at the University of Virginia. She never forgot that the woman who had carried her in her womb was out there somewhere, and the thought warmed her heart to the extent that she never felt alone.

Angie led Scarlett across the clearing to the Bogeyman. She pointed up at the towering structure. Its ominous shape was taking form. "It's meant to celebrate the coming of spring on the first day of May during a festival called Beltane. It's something Mr. Gant learned when he lived in Ireland where they burned them as some sort of sacrifice. It sounds sort of scary, don't it?"

Angie was ready to move on but Scarlett moved closer to the wicker creature. She had seen a drawing in a college text about druids from pre-Christian times, but the enormity and raw aspect of the structure was frightening. Then she recalled the drawing. Humans were jailed inside and burned alive! Scarlett's imagination had momentarily imposed itself on her reasoning. The whole scene was eerie. She was glad when they moved on.

"This here is where Mr. Gant lives with his girlfriend," Angie said, and pointed to a cabin that had recently been enlarged. She added after a short pause, "And meets with the people he controls. Over there," she pointed to another cabin, "is where some of the workers stay, and over to the right there's a camping area with tents for us guys who are living here, but they've got some barracks they say they're going to let us who stay move into."

"But you don't have to stay here, do you?" Scarlett asked.

Angie moved close to Scarlett. She began to whisper, "Where do you think most of us girls could find a place? Some of the men, too? It's like the Moonies. Mr. Gant collects the money we make and gives us an allowance. Some of us came here just to let our hair down and celebrate in a new scene. Now we're far from home and trapped." Angie moved so her nose almost touched Scarlett's face, "You got a way to get home, you run, girl," she said.

The forest became deeper as they walked. They came to a stream bordered on both sides by lush foliage. The bubbling water whispered to them as it flowed over pebbles and stones polished by time and the force of nature.

They continued along the stream until they reached a fence. "This is as far as we are allowed to go," Angie said. "See the sign over there?"

The sign said "Private Property. Do not enter."

"What's back there? Scarlett said.

"They say there's some kind of place like a jail, but nobody seems to know." Angie began to turn around when a man blocked the path.

"Hello Angie," the man said. "What brings you back here?"

Angie's voice began to falter and fade until it was just a jumble of words. It was obvious she was deathly afraid of him.

"Mister Gant, sir, I, we, trying to sh, sh, show Red here around. I, I'm, sorry if we come too far." The remainder of what she said trailed off until Scarlett could hardly hear a syllable.

Victor Gant took Angie's arm and Scarlett could see the pressure his thumb was making but his voice remained calm. "Dear Angie, you know we don't come back here. Take your friend, Red, and go back to work on the project up front. There's still a lot to be done."

Vincent Gower turned his eyes to look at Red, and Scarlett turned to face him. She removed her hood. Her strawberry hair fell out. She had placed a sprig with dogwood blossoms in her hair. Her face was pale with light freckles. She was nothing like the other girls. She was stunning. Vincent's heart skipped a beat. An unholy feeling came over him. He seemed to be caught in a scene from the past—one that tore at his guts. "Good Lord, I've seen her before," he thought. "Where, where?"

"Red, I hope you will join us as we head toward a glorious celebration marking the coming of spring," he said in a shaky voice. "Please be sure to join me in my cabin on your way back. I want to know more about you. Angie will show you the way."

Angie clutched Scarlett's arm as they scampered back along the trail. Scarlett made an excuse to break away and used a small transmitter and code to inform her contact outside the Hollow, who then keyed Washington and the superior she only knew as Sam. "He goes by the name Victor Gant," she said. "He's about six feet, and there's something odd about his face. The skin is stretched tight while his neck and arms are that of an older man. Looks like plastic surgery. Lots of wiry hair, dyed black, but salt and pepper underneath. A smile that pulls to the left because of what's been done to his face. Lots of muscle in his arms and upper body, and his fingerprints have obviously been altered. Agent's observation from proximity: Cruel and evil looking and in firm control. All aimed toward a Mayday festival with ominous overtones. I'll report again tomorrow." But she never did. Sam pulled her out immediately. After all the years of pursuing him, Sam thought they had finally found Vincent Gower.

QUINT

Quinton Parker stood before Mother Superior Mary Celeste's gilded throne. Mother Superior sat without moving, whispering to the black dog on her lap that had started a low-pitched growl. The dog soon fell quiet, and Mary Celeste gave Quint a fleeting smile.

"Don't you have a name for him yet?" Quint asked.

"The sisters and I couldn't settle on a name so we're still calling him 'Doge' with the 'e' thrown in to give it some class. He likes it, but I know it's too impersonal. We're trying to stay away from a Saint's name. He's not that kind of dog. You can take a hand at naming him if you like."

Quint grunted a no thank you, and Mary Celeste took her eyes off the dog, frowning as she considered what to say. She bent her head and hesitated as the color rose in her cheeks. She was doing something she was uncomfortable with. "Quint, the reason I sent for you is because I wanted to find out how you're doing with what we were talking about. You remember," she said, "getting the admissions matter settled for my niece, Sharon?"

Quint raised his hand to get her attention and drew her eyes to him.

"Look, I did what we both thought was the right thing to do," he said. The Bishop is aware she shouldn't be here posing as a nun, and it's only temporary; but if I hadn't done something, she would soon be back in the mental institution. Our people at the FBI who investigate this kind of thing are pretty sure Sharon never should have been there in the first place, and probably wouldn't if the DA hadn't had a tough re-election fight. But to answer your question, I'm using all the influence I have with my contacts, and I believe I have it handled, but you know how the admissions people at some of these church schools can be."

Sharon was the daughter of Mary Celeste's sister Sarah, and stepdaughter of US Senator Ben Porter. In Hanover, where it was a topic of conversation that never seemed to die, folks discussed the injustice in incarcerating Senator Porter's stepdaughter for most of her young life on what many thought was shoddy evidence. They were convinced the evidence was presented in a way to stir up resentment towards her grandfather, Buck Tindal, the unyielding and incorruptible retired County sheriff who had kept himself involved in politics. When Ben, the WWII Medal of Honor hero, was elected to the US Senate, he brought immediate attention to the case. Sharon was soon released into the temporary care of Mary Celeste at Our Lady of Perpetual Help.

Quint could see Mary Celeste beginning to stiffen. "Look," he attempted to placate her, "with your assurances, Sharon should be able to enroll within a few days, but a few days could stretch into a week or more. It wouldn't be good for you to get a visit from someone outside the Church. Here's what I suggest. Let her stay here this weekend. First of the week, whether we have her enrolled or not, I'll take her down to Chattanooga and let her shop for school clothes; then she can stay at my place until the school calls. Maybe she can spend some down time with her brother."

Quint Parker was somewhat over six feet, but because a bomb explosion while trying to shut down a drug cartel left him unable to fully stand erect, he looked shorter. His face was oval and nondescript in a way that wouldn't stand out in a crowd when he was on assignment. Quint had a special relationship with Mother Superior Mary Celeste. She had become his Confessor.

Quint had returned to his Alma Mater on the 'Mountain' not long after another horrific event had finished his career with the FBI. The way he told it, sitting in a chair before her with his hands together as if in prayer, moved Mary Celeste to bend forward to enclose his hands in hers.

"We were returning from a family vacation to the Bahamas. Because of my assignments, we hadn't had one together in a while, but we had a great time and the girls learned to snorkel in water that was so clear you couldn't be afraid. When we got back to Miami, we had to rush to make our connections. I remember hurrying with my wife, Stella, and the girls, Katie and Margo, to the departure gate, and we were the last to make it through before they closed the doors. I," he paused. "I kissed them all good-by. It was the last time I saw them."

Quint started to sob, sucking air into his lungs with racking spasms. He couldn't finish the story, but he didn't have to. Mary Celeste had heard the rest. Quint would be catching a later flight back to Washington to report for another assignment. Almost immediately after takeoff, a freak fire broke out in a lower compartment under the passenger section of the plane Stella and the girls were on. The fire fed rapidly on combustible packing. Out of control, it engulfed the compartment and burned through the plane's flight controls. The jet crashed in the Everglades. All 201 aboard were killed.

Mary Celeste had also heard what happened later. The tragedy ruined Quint. He started to drink and it began to show. He could not be consoled. His mouth was sealed and lips drawn. He was a mess and everyone knew it. When he could no longer contain his grief and be effective at work, Quint walked into the Director's office and resigned.

Mary Celeste moved around the desk to face Quint. For the first time in her life she took a man in her arms and cried with him, unable to contain her own grief.

On one particular morning of the anniversary of his family's death when he was in the grip of a gnawing emptiness, Quint returned once again to the convent to talk with Mary Celeste. When he stood before her with all his grief bottled up, Mary Celeste knew what she had to do. She pulled back the scarf covering her head to reveal the slot of the severed ear and the scar from the tip down her neck to the swell above her breast, leaving the rest to his imagination.

"Do you know my story?" she asked abruptly.

"Yes, I know about it," he said. "I am so sorry."

"Well, then you know that I lost something also, a baby girl that they took from my body and who is out there somewhere. You see Quint, running this convent with all the dysfunctional nuns who identify with me is what the Church wants from me. In a way, it has become the cross we all have to bear. They can't leave and neither can I. So unless my child finds me, I will never get to see her. So you need to get on with your life, Quint. It may sound heartless, but if you are to survive, that is what you must do. That is what I had to do."

Quint straightened up. He looked at Mary Celeste. He tried to say something but couldn't. He turned and slowly walked away. What would it be like if his wife and kids had walked away from the plane crash and he was so incapacitated he couldn't find them? He was unaware at the time of how his pain would help Mary Celeste.

SWEET SEPTEMBER

Megan Pappas was a girl with a bad habit. She couldn't say "No." It wasn't about sex though. She'd thought a lot about it, but sex wasn't a step she was ready to take. But almost everything else was. "Megan, would you do this for me?" or "Megan, can you babysit tonight?" almost always got a nod.

She lived across the street from Matthew Porter's grandmother, Rebecca Porter; and one sweet September day when Matt visited, Megan had been alongside her mother who was talking with Mrs. Porter. Matt immediately sized Megan up, and walked towards her with the poised step of someone who was accustomed to approaching females of all ages. As Matt and Megan came face to face he gave her a smile that was more than just an ordinary splash on his face.

Megan, who had been raised on tasty Greek recipes and was overweight, blushed. She was just a freshman in high school then, but every time Matt visited his grandmother and she saw him, Megan found an excuse to cross the street and position herself where he would have to notice her. Megan was in a real quandary. She knew about Matthew Porter's reputation with girls. How was a sweet, innocent high school freshman going to get him to take the next step? She couldn't resist fantasizing about it. She just couldn't!

Matthew was the son of the junior senator from North Carolina, Ben Porter, who was best known for his 'David and Goliath' duel in the swamp that caught international attention; and if that wasn't enough, he was the grandson of Buck Tindal, the legendary sheriff of Hanover County. Matt was a physically fit high school senior with broad shoulders tapering to a narrow waist. At an even six feet, he had brown hair and light blue eyes so pale they reminded one of a field of cotton after a touch of summer rain—all attributes set on a pallet of skin the color of lightly browned toast from his summer job as a lifeguard.

Then Matt was off to college, and Megan rarely saw him again until she enrolled in the same college three years later when he was a senior; and hadn't it been a coincidence to run into him in the Student Union that first week in September and have him show her where her English class was being held. When Matt stopped Megan one day and asked if she would like to go to his fraternity party and dance, she almost died but held it inside, smiled, and said yes. It wasn't like being invited to the Senior Class Graduation Dance, but it was a good start.

So here she was living in a small wooden two-story apartment building putting the finishing touches on her makeup and dressing for the evening. When she viewed herself in the mirror, she was pleased. The baby fat and extra pounds she had carried in high school were gone, and before her stood an attractive, poised young woman readying herself for the man she was already intent on marrying even if it did involve breaking a few rules about intimacy she had set for herself.

The tap, tap, tap on the door came as a surprise. It was not the stout knock that she anticipated from the most popular man on campus. But when Megan opened the door anyway, the smile she had prepared disappeared. The light in the hall had been turned off. Who was this strange-looking thin girl with long and stringy brown hair that fell to her waist, dressed in a coarse wool cloak?

That's when Megan made a bad mistake. She stepped forward to get a better look at who was standing before her. Megan never knew what hit her. The voltage from the stun gun cut her legs out from under her. Her body went into spasms, her face a mass of twitches and terror. She was on her hands and knees, trying to get up. Then the shock came again. She collapsed, paralyzed. Megan was unaware of what the girl who took a serrated knife from her bag was going to do as she followed the detailed instructions of a tall man who stood in the shadows.

"Too bad that Matt Porter wasn't here to open the door," the tall man said.

THE MESSAGE

The day my Aunt Mary told me I was going to be able to leave Our Lady of Perpetual Help, I was caught up in a state of ecstasy. Free! I was going free after all this time. As soon as I left her office, I exclaimed 'yes' in a low voice, and pumped my fist. Two nuns walking down the hall as they returned to their rooms turned to stare at me with disapproving frowns. I knew the Our Lady was in a period of silent meditation, but I was too happy to keep quiet.

Of course the sisters had no idea that I was the Mother Superior's niece or that I had spent the best years of my youth in three places—a prison, a mental institution, and as a last resort, this remote convent, which was part of an agreement with the Aunt Mary leading to my release into her care.

On an evening that would change the course of my life, I returned late for the beginning of Compline, the ending prayer service of the evening. One of my duties as a supposed Postulant was to check all entrances and exits to verify that they were properly secured, and, as often as not, I was held up by other responsibilities assigned to me. As I shimmied my way onto the hard wood bench of the chapel behind twelve sisters grasping their rosaries, Mother Superior Mary Celeste gave me a brief but pointed glance of displeasure for interrupting the service.

I tried to follow along but fidgeted, and at the dismissal, immediately slipped out and hurried to my small room on the second floor of the convent. This was to be one of my last nights here. I was aware that I was smiling, which was rare for me these days. I didn't care how the man named Quint was making it happen, but I was supposed to be enrolled in the local college within the next few days. As I packed my few belongings, I heard a noise at the window. I thought it was the scraping of a branch caught by the wind howling around the granite edges of this forlorn and ghostly building. But then it came again and again with a telltale impact. I decided to investigate, and walked to a narrow slot in the wall and began to crank open the single paned leaded window. The squeak of seldom-used metal on metal scratched the surface of the evening like chalk on a blackboard. A pebble landed nearby, and I looked down. Out of nowhere I heard a hoarse whisper carried on the wind, and I recognized the voice.

"Sharon! It's Matt. I need to see you!"

The quietness that followed his words fell like a door closing out the sounds of the night.

"Matt? What are you doing here this time of the evening? We're in lockdown and silence."

"Something horrible has happened," he moaned. "I need to see you now."

"Okay, okay, just give me a few minutes," I said.

I pulled on my threadbare, quilted robe and slipped out an exit to descend on an old rusty fire escape. As soon as I reached the ground I came face to face with my younger half-brother. We fixed our eyes on each other. His face was twisted in pain. For the first time in years, we had the opportunity to reach out and touch each other.

"Megan," he began without preface, "who was supposed to

be my date tonight, has been assaulted. I found her. She was stripped and whoever did it took a knife to her. They cut her ear and part of her breast, and did something horrible to her pubic area, for God's sake! She's been taken to a trauma unit in Chattanooga. I tried to help her and got blood on my hands and shirt. The police have been questioning me. They think I did it!"

The relationship between Matt and me had been strained by an event in the past, but if there were anyone he would trust, it would be me, despite the fact I had once been diagnosed as a murdering psychopath.

I listened in horror at what Matt had discovered, especially the severing of Megan's body parts. I knew about it from something that had happened to Mary Celeste a long time ago.

"We have to tell Aunt Mary now," I said. "Come to the front entrance quick. I'll let you in."

Mary Celeste settled in the gilded chair and waited for the knock at the door. Sharon was late with the lock-down report so perhaps there was a problem. When the tap, tap, tap came, the black dog growled. She hushed him, left the chair and cracked the door. Sharon entered and stood nervously before the Mother Superior. Sharon was an inch over six feet with broad sloping shoulders. Her face was heart shaped with one side slightly off center as if the artist who had made the cast had been careless. When you got accustomed to the discrepancy, you might even say she was beautiful with her nearly ink-purple eyes, upturned pert nose and full sensuous mouth.

"What's wrong, Sharon?" Mary Celeste asked. She had never seen her so edgy before.

"Aunt Mary, something terrible has happened over at the college. Matt's date was assaulted and cut up pretty bad. Matt found her. The police think he did it. He's outside the door."

Mary Celeste moved until her body was up close to Sharon. "You know how to address me," she whispered. "Please don't ever call me 'Aunt' again. This group of sisters is in a place where they can't get out. If they ever find out you're my niece and getting special treatment, they could riot and take over the convent. As it is, it's only my appearance of power that keeps the twelve in line. Now bring Matt in."

Mary Celeste retreated to the gilded chair. The dog sat beside her.

Matt nodded to her as he entered. He had not seen her recently, but she held herself in a kind of regal stance, and the beauty from photos taken years ago that he had seen was still evident in her face.

When Matt told Mary Celeste what had happened, her face went white and her hands began to shake.
"Oh, God, please, say Vincent hasn't come back," she said and put her arm around the black dog whose hackles rose, and he started to growl.

PART FOUR

VOICES

SHARON'S VOICE

Things never seem to work out as planned. When Aunt Mary told Quint Parker what happened to Megan, and that it was like the same thing that happened to her, he immediately called the local sheriff, Rob Brinkley. He asked for 24-hour surveillance of the area around Our Lady of Perpetual Help, and he got it. Then I heard him talk to the FBI in Washington, and it seemed like he knew the person he was talking to and he didn't mince any words.

After that, he surprised Mary Celeste and me by announcing that he was going to spend the night at Our Lady. We weren't going to leave until the campus, that was now on lockdown, had been searched and the police had either caught the assailant or were confident that the person was no longer in the area. It was obvious that Quint's training had kicked in and he was now in charge.

The next morning he met with Sheriff Brinkley and his deputies and talked to the FBI again, and in the afternoon he declared it was time to leave Our Lady and move on to his house. I hugged and kissed Aunt Mary, and left it to her to explain what was happening.

As we walked to his car from the convent, I could see he was carrying a handgun in a holster attached to his belt, and he could see I was looking at it. He cracked a small side-of-the mouth smile, and I understood he was telling me not to be afraid; and that even though it looked sort of sinister and out of place, it was only there to protect me.

When we got to his place, I had a chance to look him over carefully as we walked up the winding path to his house. The surgeries following the explosion that damaged him had left him slightly bent at the waist so it looked as if he was permanently crunching his muscles, but he still moved up the incline to his house without difficulty.

He was a handsome man, or had been once. What stood out to me about him were his slate grey eyes. It was like you were looking at a piece of polished stone that somehow had come alive. The other thing was his face, which without saying a word told an old story. It was something to watch.

His house was small, and really not more than a cottage set on the lip of the mountain. It had two adjacent bedrooms that shared a bathroom, a combination living room-dining room next to a kitchen, a small study, and an uncovered porch on the back looking out and down into the valley. It was a man's house with none of the frilly stuff some women might have—just pine furniture, throw rugs, a steel gun safe, fishing rods stuck in the corner, that kind of thing.

Quint sat me down and told me what he expected. "First of all, we've got to get you dressed like a coed and acting like a student. You're big, let's face it. I don't mean fat, just big. I've got an old pair of jeans you can probably get into and a hunting type shirt that will fit, anything to get you out of that nun's habit. The FBI's got a female agent in Chattanooga who'll help you get dressed like the other students and teach you how to conduct yourself when you're with them. I've talked with your brother, Matt, and he's going to fill you in on some other stuff, and then," Quint chuckled, "I think we'll be ready to show you off to the world."

When it was time for bed, and I was under the covers pretending to sleep, I started thinking about how Quint must feel if he thought there was an insane, bloodthirsty psychopath lurking in the next room just waiting until he fell asleep to strike. I joked with him about it the next day as we sat across the breakfast table from one another, and he asked me if I wanted to talk about it. I said yes because I needed to get on with my life. I knew I wasn't going back to the convent.

We never had coffee at Our Lady, but Quint had made a pot and it smelled so good that I followed what he did and mixed in cream and sugar and brought it to the table. Quint's slate grey eyes were fixed on me, and I closed mine while I tried to find a place in memory to begin my story. When I finally found my voice, I began:

It was hard growing up knowing that a madman who heard voices that drove him to violence sired me. I knew he raped my mother and murdered several people, and that's always haunted me. Mom and Ben Porter, the man I now call dad, tried to keep my life as normal as possible, but you know how talk gets around in a small town, and I got a lot of attention especially growing up as big as I was, and with my father's reputation hanging around my neck like a noose.

Two things came together like a perfect storm. Actually, three. When I reached puberty, I sometimes believed I actually heard voices, especially at night when I was trying to sleep and the house was quiet. I thought maybe I inherited it from my birth father and was going insane like him. I told my mom and she said it was just my imagination, but she looked worried and took me to a psychologist. I started seeing her on a regular basis, and she had me take a number of tests. Finally, she told mom that she could find no evidence of mental illness, but that the voices were probably due to my extremely vivid imagination and would go away as I grew older. However, I should be closely observed to see if 'the voices' continued. What happened next just added fuel to the fire.

One day at the boathouse when I was talking with Matt, I told him about it, and you've met Matt, he's a few years younger than me, and he said I was crazy. That hurt me, and I decided to play a joke on him. The next day I went out to the boathouse early and dropped a rod from our boat over the side. When Matt and I went out there later, I told him to dive down and look for it because it wasn't deep there and he would have enough breath to do it. My idea was to move the boat to another place in the boathouse where it would be partly concealed, so when he came up with the rod he wouldn't see it right away and I'd be in the boat and start laughing until he found me.

Like I said, things don't ever seem to work out the way you plan them, and just as I had untied the bow and stern lines and started to pull the boat along the catwalk to a dark mooring at its end, the worst thing happened. I heard a loud noise and slapping on the water from a powerboat racing down the channel. As it approached you could hear the revving of the outboard motor. It was closing on the boathouse as if it was in a game of chicken to see how close the driver could come. And then it was gone, and in a moment the wake left behind hit the boathouse and surged inside forcing the rail of our boat under the catwalk so that it was overlapping it like a lip. I was knocked down by the impact and soaked by the waves as they continued their turbulence. I knew Matt was trapped somewhere underneath the fusion of the boat and the catwalk. I got up and steadied myself against the continued rocking. I found an oar and wedged it between the boat and the catwalk using the oar as leverage. The boat would not budge so I stood as close to the submerged side as possible so that my weight forced it down, and finally as I continued to push with the oar, the boat floated free, and Matt burst to the surface. He was gasping for air and sheer panic was still on his face. He was so mad his face turned blood red, and he began to accuse me of trying to drown him. Finally, he started to run toward the house.

"I'm going to tell Mom and Dad what you did," he shouted at me as he raced down the length of the pier. I tried to convince my parents what happened was just an accident, but they kept questioning me about it. I don't think they ever believed me. That was the first event, and together with another that was to come, got me where I am today.

Gilmer White

One year, I think I was fourteen, but I remember it was after I reached puberty and while I was seeing the psychologist, and after the thing with Matt. It was summer and school was out, and I was staying in town with Ben Porter's mother, whom we all affectionately called Miss Becky, while Ben and Mom were on some kind of government-sponsored trip. As the Junior Senator from North Carolina, he traveled a lot and Mom liked to go with him whenever she could. Just so you know, I had always considered myself a Porter so my family consisted of my mother, Sarah, my stepdad, Ben, Ben's daughter, Rachel, whose mother had died tragically in the swamp, and, of course, Matt, who is Ben and Sarah's child. It was quite a mixture, but we loved each other, and like most families, with the exception a few hitches, we got along together fine.

It was Sunday afternoon after we got home from church and Miss Becky was cooking and old sheriff Tindal who was married to her was asleep in a big stuffed chair. He and I talked to each other a lot and he once confided in me and told about a girl named Marie whom he left behind in France after World War I. He said she was a nurse in a hospital, and after he was wounded and disabled, she took care of him. He talked about her when he had a drink or two, and I got the picture that they had lived together and were very happy. I think he felt regret or guilt or both that he had left her behind as he had an old battered snapshot of her he kept in his wallet. It showed a pretty girl standing in a vineyard with a splash of sunlight on her face.

Matt was pretending to help Miss Becky cook, and I had just put down a book and was feeling restless, so I decided to take a walk. Miss Becky had never moved from the old house on 6th Street and it was located in a neighborhood that had begun to seriously run down. Most of the old families had moved on, but she had memories she couldn't let go of, some good and some bad, so she had stayed, and one year ran into the next and so on until there she was living in both the past and the present. You could see she had finally come to terms with a house that had a strange history attached to it.

After explaining to Miss Becky that I was going out, I left through the front door, but because there was a rumble of thunder stepped back inside. And that, Quint, was when things began to go wrong. If I had just stayed inside, I wouldn't be in the fix I'm in today. Instead, I went to a hall closet to get a small umbrella. On a peg hung a hunting knife in a sheath, and as I stood there looking at it, I thought wasn't it strange for a hunting knife to just be hanging there. It struck me as somehow sinister. The sheath had been rubbed with some kind of polish and the handle of the knife had the look of something that had been used many times. I don't know how to explain it but my imagination was drawn to that knife like it might be to a painting in a gallery, and for a moment I was the person in the painting with that knife. Wouldn't it be nice just to hold it and make the scene look real? I stood transfixed by my imagination and finally slipped the sheath off the peg and pushed it inside the umbrella case.

"It wasn't raining when I left the house again, so I started down the block for what I thought would be a short walk. There was an old three-story house on the next block that had been deserted as long as anyone could remember. It had been condemned, but somehow the city hadn't done anything about it. It just stood there like a beacon to the past with yellow tape around it.

"When I had walked as far as the old house, I stopped. It once had been painted grey, then much later, yellow, and now both layers were peeling. Most of the shutters were missing and some hung by a single bracket. It was just an old, dilapidated, lost-in-time kind of house.

"I was about to move on when the rain started coming down hard. Instead of being stranded with the umbrella, I crossed under the yellow tape and stepped onto the porch. It was strewn with the debris of a house that was falling apart. From some past time, possibly a Halloween, was a sign still hanging with the inscription, HAUNTED HOUSE. I crossed the porch and entered through a doorframe without a door. I could hear the rain pounding down, and I stood there smelling the staleness of the house.

When the rain shower had passed over, I was getting ready

to leave when I saw two young men standing in the doorframe, and I thought they were there for the same reason I was. They were dressed in dirty shirts and jeans and stood there smiling at me.

"I'm just getting ready to leave," I told them.

"Don't do that. Stay and keep us company," the taller one with the stained beard said.

"I live up the street in the house with Sheriff Tindal and I have to go," I said with emphasis on the Sheriff's name.

"She lives with the Sheriff, Luke," the tall one said, mocking me.

Luke was shorter, and even at his age had begun to go bald. He had a scar on his face and mean yellow eyes.

"The sheriff!" he laughed derisively. "He's so old he probably can't get it up anymore."

I knew I was in trouble. "I've got to go," I repeated, and moved towards the door.

"Don't rush off, little darling," the tall one said, and grabbed me.

"What do you think, Luke?" he asked, and pressed himself against me.

"Shit, Crow, I don't know. She looks a little young for the kind of stuff you like to do."

I could hear Crow breathing and the pressure from his crotch as he moved his arms around my breasts.

Quint, I swear I don't know how I had the strength to break out of Crow's grasp, but I did, and started to run, but the guy named Luke had his arms spread out like this, and was blocking me. We all just stood there for a moment, still, not moving, with me between the two of them. I suddenly remembered the knife and reached inside the umbrella cover and drew it out. It was wicked looking with a hook on the front of the blade like they use in dressing an animal.

"Leave me alone!" I yelled kind of hoping someone would be passing by and hear me.

Crow laughed and moved towards me. I remember he said, "Now, honey, you know you ain't gonna use that. Drop it and come to daddy."

He inched towards me with his arm outstretched like he

wanted to take my hand, and suddenly he lunged, and I hit him with the knife. I could feel it sink in, and when he stumbled up to me I looked dead into his eyes and there was a look of disbelief in them. Just then one of his feet began to beat on the floor as if he were trying to stop the pain. Then he began to slide down, and as he did his weight pulled the knife with the hook out, and you could hear a ripping sound as he sank to the floor. Blood was everywhere. Luke was at my shoulder and I swung around and slashed the knife at him, but he pulled back and the knife only cut through his clothing and skin.

"You crazy bitch," he yelled, and I guess I was. He ran out the open door and I ran out behind him screaming like a Banshee. I took off up the middle of the street towards home, and then the terror of what had happened hit me, and I collapsed. When someone spotted me and stopped, I was gasping for air, soaked in Crow's blood, and had a bloody knife in my hand.

With my genetic history and psychological background plus my father, Luther's, murderous rampage, and Luke's lying testimony that I came at them unprovoked with a knife, one that turned out to come from Miss Becky's house, I ended up in a prison, then a mental institution, and finally in the convent.

I stopped to catch my breath before I blurted out, "Now tell me about yourself, Quint."

QUINT'S VOICE

The right side of Quint's face around his eye began to twitch and he put his hand to his face to control it. Aunt Mary had confided to me that he often responded to contact from women and children that way, and as I looked into his eyes, I could see his pain. Quint gave me an expression between a half grin and a grimace and left the room. When he returned his eyes were red. I felt miserable. I knew I had gone too far in asking about his past.

"Going to Chattanooga," was all he said. "Get your things together and fix yourself up best you can."

When I returned he was standing at the front door. His truck was idling outside. As we started down the mountain Quint cleared his throat and began:

I don't talk much about what happened anymore. It doesn't help anything. Except for my early life, there's not a hell of a lot to tell beyond what you probably already know.

I was born on Knott's Island, North Carolina, which is split between North Carolina and Virginia. My family has lived there for more than a century, and I still have cousins there. We were dirt poor. Before I came along, my dad scraped out a living as a hunting and fishing guide, but the family was always going without, and if it hadn't been for some neighbors and the folks at the local Episcopal Church, I don't know how we would have made it.

Let's see. I almost forgot. We had two Chesapeake Bay Retrievers. With their thick coats and endurance, they could take the freezing weather better during duck hunting season than most of the other breeds. My dad would take me with him sometimes, and I remember the bone cold, teeth chattering days on the water with him and the dogs. I've been planning to get a Chessie for myself, and when everything settles down, that's what I'm going to do. I really miss having a dog and some other things too.

My mom was from Norfolk, and when her family came over for a tour, she met my dad and fell for him. Her family had a lot of money and mine didn't, and that ultimately turned out to be the problem after they got married. My sister and I came along in short order, and when I look back on it, it seemed we were a happy family. In the end, however, my mom couldn't stand the isolation and the poverty that surrounded her, and she took my sister and returned to Norfolk. I still remember the nights I cried myself to sleep. She's still alive and when I'm in Norfolk, I always visit her and I can tell she feels bad about what happened. My sister, she got married to some rich real-estate guy and she has four children, all girls. I see her once in a while but we're not close. Anyway, I grew up mostly around men except for my grandmother who was the only woman at home after my mom left. She taught me a lot about life and the respect you had to have for others. It almost killed me when she died.

To cut it short, because of my mom's dad, who turned out to be a pretty regular guy, I got a scholarship at the college here, and he paid my way to law school, and then the FBI liked my background and picked me up. After the plane crash, I could never get my life back together, and I ended up back on the mountain. So there you have it.

I didn't say anything, and as we headed down the mountain, I looked at all the trees that had already shed most of their fall and winter colors and then down at the ominous depth and shadows of the valley. When we came to the bottom of the mountain and hit the straightaway, there were fields being plowed for spring planting, and a few old fields with withering corn stalks reminding me of last year's cruel winter. "See Rock City" signs began to appear on the pitched red roofs of barns as well as directions to Lookout Mountain. When we reached the outskirts of Chattanooga, Quint kept to a curve in the highway where a ridge ran like a lip around the city. In some of the neighborhoods you could see quilts being hung by the road for sale, and at one stand there was a man blowing glass and making vases and jugs and things like that. He soon turned off into a development that looked as if it was in a state of transition with older homes at one end and new construction at the other and with "For Sale" signs in both. He circled the neighborhood scanning it as if he were an eagle looking for prey and finally came to a house with several gables that looked much the same as some of the others, but different in a way I couldn't understand at the time.

Quint parked the car down the street on the other side and we walked back and stood before a door that looked like it was made of solid oak. He pushed a single button on a box with a lot of buttons, and when the intercom came on, he said, "Fox," and after several minutes the door opened. Before us stood a woman who looked like someone's secretary with horn rimmed glasses, and that kind of look that had a question attached to it. Quint looked at her as if he hadn't seen her in a long while and seemed pleased with what he saw.

"Quint," she said, and ran her eyes over him, and gave him something between a hug and a firm embrace.

"Kay," he said, and acted like he didn't know how to respond, and finally put his arms around her, and that was their greeting. The whole scene seemed odd, and it dawned on me that what I was about to observe unfolding was another painful chapter in Quint's life.

Kay was probably in her early forties. She was tall and trim and wore a tailored skirt and white blouse with translucent buttons and a tiny gold cross at her throat. Her hair looked like it was naturally blond with only a few strands of grey, and it was styled in a way so that it framed her face but was gathered in back. I could see a small hearing aid attached to her left ear. Her green eyes quickly turned to me.

"This is Sharon," he said as he took my arm and moved me to the front. It was obvious they had already talked about me.

"Hello, pleased to meet you," I said, and Kay took my hand in hers and smiled.

Quint and Kay excused themselves while I sat in a study that looked like a doctor's waiting room. When they reappeared, Quint seemed sort of lost.

"I'll be back in a couple of days," he said. "Kay here will teach you what you need to know."

That's all he said, and with Kay and I standing together, he half turned like he was going to say something else, but whatever it was must have been lost, because he turned back and headed towards his truck. I must have had a puzzled look on my face as I turned to Kay because she seemed to consider something carefully before she spoke.

KAY'S VOICE

"You look like you need to know what's going on," Kay said, "so I'm going to tell you something that I hope you'll keep between the two of us?"

I nodded and she began:

You've heard about what happened to cripple Quint. I was one of the team with him on the raid when the bomb went off. Quint and two other agents crashed the door of the drug house and went in. I was on the porch when the explosion went off. The entry way had been wired. Both of my eardrums were ruptured by the explosion, but I got up and managed to get back on the porch and crawled inside the house and found Quint and the other two agents. I couldn't do anything for them, but went to work on Quint, and talked to him and told him to hold on, look at me, and stay conscious.

We had a close relationship up until then. Took vacations together, even talked about getting married. I visited him in the hospital as often as I could until I got transferred. The visits were torture for both of us. His recovery would take a long time, maybe up to a year or two before he could be operational, if ever. After a short medical stay to repair my hearing, I was reassigned. The time had come when I had to get on with my life, and so did he. I met Stella at the hospital and knew he was in good hands, so I felt fine about how it turned out for him until the plane crash, and what happened afterwards. When I met him after that I knew he would never be the same again, but we have remained close because of the life we once shared.

After explaining her past, Kay showed me to my room. Later, we had a formal dinner with other members of the staff, and I learned some things about table manners that I had forgotten over the years because nobody in the mental institution or prison practiced anything, and the nuns were so uptight they were like chickens pecking feed.

One of the people at the table was a beautiful woman with strawberry red hair. Her name was Scarlett O'Quinn. She said she was from Washington, and that she had just joined the staff in Chattanooga. She was going to share time with Kay in getting me ready for school. We smiled at each other.

The next morning Scarlett took me to an upscale dress shop, and I got fitted with everything a girl would ever need including stuff she wouldn't. Scarlett was so patient with me and took time to explain when to wear what. Next, she took me to a salon where they shampooed and styled my hair and shaped my eyebrows. Then, we had lunch in a quiet café, and that's when my curiosity got the best of me and I asked her, "How did you come to join the FBI? I mean, you've got the looks to be a movie star."

SCARLETT'S VOICE

Scarlett laughed before answering my question: "There's a story behind the 'movie star' rumors, and it happens to involve a real movie star. Do you remember catching some old flicks with an up and coming Spanish starlet named Angel Miranda? Well, the man I worked for, the famous attorney, Val Bruce, was in Hollywood on business. They met at a party and immediately hit it off. He pursued her even showing up on many of her sets. They soon became a celebrated twosome—one seldom seen without the other. Most people thought it was destined to be one of the few great Hollywood marriages. Tragically, she was killed in an auto accident with him at the wheel. He never got over it, never married, and threw all his energies into his work. Today, he heads the most prestigious law firm in Washington.

"Well, my dad works for his firm. They met abroad and became close friends, and he became like a member of our family since he didn't have one of his own. I've known him forever. He was my Godfather when I was baptized, and stood for my vows until I could take them myself at Confirmation. My father said Val once told him I reminded him of Angel. Anyway, when I finished college, he became my mentor, and coached me through law school and hired me when I came out. He's always known I was adopted, and has put himself and his firm behind trying to locate my birth mother. Still does, but due to a fire where the adoption papers were held, and the Church stonewalling on revealing any more info, the trail has been lost. It hurt me to leave his firm and go to work for the FBI, but it was my best chance of using my new skills to find my birth mom. That's the most important thing in the world for me."

Scarlett rose from the table and it was obvious she would say no more. I thought I was finished with instruction until the next morning but she took me to a dance studio to learn some basic dance steps. Afterwards, we sat in the foyer of the FBI Safe House with Kay waiting for Quint. Scarlett was notified she had a phone call and excused herself.

I was dressed in a plaid skirt, calf-high black boots, and a green jacket over a long-sleeved white blouse, and when Quint arrived, he puckered up his lips and whistled. Kay and I smiled.

I knew then how much Kay and I meant to him, but how we would probably never be an intimate part of his life.

PART FIVE

DANCE OF
THE DRUIDS

BROKEN RELICS

he night the story of my life turned yet another page, I lay in my bed at Our Lady, Doge lying on the floor next to me, dreading the task of once again trying to find sleep. The attack on Megan had gotten under my skin to the point that I began to worry about being on the brink of another panic attack. As I tried to practice the positive techniques the therapist had taught, I began to hyperventilate instead.

Then the past came back with a vengeance. It was difficult to believe that Vincent might still be out there; that he still wanted to possess a body he had already destroyed; that he might be lurking nearby. To get my mind off myself I began to pray for poor Megan. I could not help but visualize the violence that had been inflicted on her, and it caused me to pause and shudder.

I got out of bed, slipped on the robe I used for night emergencies, and went to the narrow leaded glass window and cracked it open to look out into the night. Somewhere to the east there was a shading of new light, a rooster began to crow, and the nightingale with its melodious song went quiet. It was the beginning of the terror that would haunt the rest of my life.

Around noon each day, I walk to the convent mailbox to collect the mail. It is located outside the moat so once I collect it, I take it in to my office to sort it out. Today, some of the pieces were for the sisters, others were addressed to me from the Church, and there was one letter in a plain white envelope addressed to me without any identification from the sender.

As I stuck the point of the opener into the corner a peculiar odor emerged, one that I had smelled before. What was it? I placed my nose closer to the envelope. It was the smell of formaldehyde. I finished opening the envelope and shook out onto the table two objects. One was brown and shriveled and looked like a mushroom. The other was small and oblong shaped and very wrinkled. "What?" I thought, and then it hit me. They were the missing parts of my body that could not be located after the assault almost twenty years ago.

I started to hyperventilate and was overcome by nausea and rushed to the toilet. When at last I recovered from the shock of seeing those grotesque objects, I called Quint's number praying every second as the phone rang that he would be in. When he finally answered all I could think to blurt out was "Quint, come quick!"

Before I could fully collect myself, three cars, two with blue lights flashing, skidded to a stop in the small parking space at the side of the convent. Four men holding guns jumped out and raced across the wooden bridge to the entrance. Even though I was filled with that old feeling of terror, at the sound of the sirens I had stepped outside to see Quint, Sheriff Brinkley, and two deputies jump from their cars. In the parking lot, the sirens from the two patrol cards were winding down.

"Thank God you're okay!" Quint exclaimed, and pushed me

inside. "Sheriff, have your men search the grounds for any suspicious activity."

Sisters were standing in the hall when we entered and I could see the curiosity on their faces. We went to my office, and I showed the contents of the envelope to Quint.

He took one look and turned to me. "Mary Celeste, you are at extreme risk," he said. "This guy, Vincent, is not going to give up. We believe he's a full-blown psychotic with some kind of agenda with you at the center. The attack on Megan was just a first step to let you know he's coming after you. The FBI has already assigned agents to the case; your brother-in-law, Senator Porter, is up-to-date on everything and is pushing the investigation; even the Church is involved. We're going to get the guy, but you've got to be careful not to expose yourself and stay inside the convent with everything locked up. We'll have someone check the locks and the security system. Sheriff Brinkley's men are patrolling the area. The point is I don't want you worrying any more than you have to."

I spent the rest of the afternoon thinking about the horror surrounding my life and the lives of others.

VALLEY OF THE DYING STARS

Vincent Gower lay on the bed in his sparsely furnished room staring with fixed, expressionless eyes at the cheap painting of a street scene in Paris on the far wall. As he flattened his body against the mattress, his image was reminiscent of an inflated parade balloon figure slowly losing air.

He had worked hard at bringing the May Day ceremonies together. The floor where the celebration would take place had been enlarged and swept clean. A Maypole, replete with ribbons and flowers, had been erected. Acquisition of and seating for musicians had been arranged. The finishing touches on the wicker and willow constructed Bogie Man had been painstakingly created so that the figure seemed to stand forebodingly over the completed theatre staging.

Vincent's vision of the climax to his personal Shakespearean tragedy was ready to be acted out. He should have been brimming over with enthusiasm, but something had upset him. The taste in his mouth was sour, and it wasn't just from the dog meat he had been chewing. The Imbas Forosna, or the knowledge that enlightens, ritual he had just completed had not gone well, and now had been complicated by the introduction of a new revelation from the leader of the Tuatha De Danaan, the pre-Christian Celtic gods who Vincent believed controlled his destiny.

"Behold, before you is a new vision from the future. You will now be joined by a captive, a woman, on your journey to the otherworld," he was told. "Your entry into the new life of the ancients now rests on your bringing the woman for whom you wish to form a union with you, and she must go through the same process of conversion as you. Should she escape while under your control you will not be reincarnated into the new life, but will drift forever in the Abyss."

The original fiery scene from his first encounter with the Tuatha De Danaan that continued to bring Vincent so much anguish sprang before his eyes once again, but now he was holding a struggling woman on the platform high at the top of Bogie. Fire had erupted below them. The woman's name now emblazoned before his eyes like a fireworks display was Mary Celeste.

Vincent forced himself to rise from the bed. He spat the piece of dog meat on the floor, beginning to sweat profusely. He had to capture Mary Celeste now. Bogie stood ready, and the May Day ceremonies were just days away.

Vincent heard the voices of the two females as they approached the room. He had interrogated both of them and was convinced that they would follow his instructions exactly as directed.

Maeve brushed through the door. Raw emotion gripped her narrow face, which was even more pinched than usual. She had become the most fanatical of all his followers. The reason was obvious: Maeve had been the only female to share his company since they left Ireland, but now there was the woman, Maggie, who wanted to be included, and all the other females who circled like vultures just waiting to take Maeve's place as "Queen of the Hill."

Maeve stood her ground by redoubling her efforts to please Vincent, and soon found herself acting out of character. She had been raised as the only girl in an orthodox druid family, which didn't believe in activities that required the sacrifice of living creatures in the May Day ceremonies. Now Vincent was insisting that she follow his instructions to the letter, including what he directed her to do to Megan Pappas.

Another of the women, Sibyl, slid through the door before Maeve could close it. Vincent knew what the problem was. They hated each other. They didn't like competition.

Sibyl was an ex Roller Derby queen from LA. She was captain of the Razors and feared by other skaters for her dirty, often violent play. She had a pretty, round face, but you could see the violence like sparks from her eyes. She was only in this Tennessee valley because her reputation caught up with her when the other teams decided to get even.

It happened when she found herself boxed in by opposing skaters. A blow from behind propelled her into a vicious elbow to the neck that put her in a hospital with a severely fractured vertebra. She was finished as a skater but not finished with the fury that drove her. She needed structure, and the Hollow was where she found it. Vincent was the only person who helped her make sense of and control the inner torment which felt like an insane person trying to kill her.

"Here is why I called you two in," Vincent said. "We've got an important job to do, and both of you have to get along if we're going to do it right. You can square off against each other later. You have to trust me and follow my instructions to the letter. It will all make sense to you later, but for now I'm asking you to do something on faith, faith in me."

The women nodded. Without hesitation Vincent continued. "We're going to break into the convent up on the mountain tonight and kidnap the nun who runs it. We're going to keep her in the stockade until the May Day ceremonies are over. I'll just add this—there are forces on the outside that want to shut down what we've taken so long to build here, and it's mainly because of the rituals we're performing as we prepare for the burning of Bogie. They're the religious fanatics who call us pagans and want us out. The person we take from the convent is the hostage I need in order to bargain with them until we complete the May Day ceremonies.

You two can remain anonymous if you wish."

The two women looked at each other and nodded. Vincent smiled. He knew what the final outcome would be, and there was something new that concerned him even in the lost morality of the druid conscience that he now avowed: Maeve was pregnant with their child. Despite everything he professed, he wanted to leave part of himself behind.

GONE

The girl with the dark purple eyes soon found herself the center of controversy. Not that she meant to be. After almost half a life spent in a mental institution, prison, and a convent, she was having a difficult time communicating in a world of college students and quizzical professors.

She smiled politely and nodded in the right places, but had the frozen appearance of being placed in a never-changing family portrait. What complicated the picture was the fact that she was an attractive girl with a flawless complexion and soft curly brown hair that framed a face with full lips and pert, upturned nose. Even the slightly misaligned left and right sides of her face called attention to her overall beauty. Of course, her physique bothered some, especially some of the more petite coeds. She was an inch over six feet with long legs, a high waist line, and a bosom that put most of her competitors to shame. But it was the impenetrable depth of her dark eyes that set her aside as a mysterious stranger come to the gate of what was once a fairly normal college, that is, until fate fouled the atmosphere and fear crept in like a hungry lion stalking a gazelle.

When Matthew Porter came forth and claimed Sharon as his sister, eyebrows were raised and both students and faculty couldn't believe that the most personable, outgoing, and accomplished senior on campus was really related to this strange girl with the same last name.

Then, Matt explained everything in a fairly logical way, "She's been in a convent and decided to leave."

Those words turned all the guys on, but Sharon wouldn't give even the most handsome and charming ones more than a polite smile. There was something else on her mind. Something Quint had told her before she moved on campus from his place .

"Vincent Gower is back for sure. What was in that envelope delivered to Mary Celeste proved it, but I think we all knew from the beginning the way Megan Pappas was cut up. We searched for him for years, but we had lost his trail and he could have walked the streets anywhere without being caught."

"They say there's a lot of strange activity in the Valley," Sharon said.

"Yeah, we're on top of it, but we don't want to spook Vincent and end up with another Jonestown," Quint said. "There are lots of young women living there now and more moving in all the time. That, in itself, has attracted an increasing number of males, including some pretty tough looking dudes. We're convinced from surveillance drugs and guns are involved, as well. DATF has a plan to raid the place and capture Vincent. Your stepfather is on top of it."

Sharon pondered on those words as she went about her activities on campus. Her natural athletic talents became evident as she practiced with the women's volleyball and soccer teams. She was the talk of the campus until something happened that changed everything.

If you had been standing there on that fateful day and saw them coming, the two of them, brother and sister, holding hands, in animated conversation, you might have thought they were lovers. But there was something else. There was a chemistry of the heart, lost for years, now like magnets pulling together the disparate parts of a family torn by grief and regret.

Once beyond the boundaries of the campus, they separated hands and walked in a rhythm found only in military and blood relationships. They walked by instinct, taking an almost obliterated trail through the forest, and through the gloaming that would soon usher in the night cries of animals that live in the high reaches of the mountains.

When they arrived at the convent, Mary Celeste was waiting.

"The sounds go on all night," she said. "The drum echoes are eerie, like something from out of Africa, and we can't close it out. Getting to sleep is difficult. The sisters are all nervous, edgy. Quint says the people down there are getting ready for a May Day celebration. Looks like the authorities in Cowan would do something to control the noise."

"There are too many people involved in the ceremonies down there to step in now," Matt said. "May Day is almost here. After that I hear they're going to close the site down."

Mary Celeste sighed.

"Let's take a look down the valley before we leave," Sharon said as she and Matt left the convent.

They walked to the edge of the mountain beyond the huge cross that now shown like a beacon to the valley below.

"It's beginning to get dark. We need more light to go any further," Matt said.

"No. We've got enough left to get as far as the ledge where the mountain begins to fall off. From there we probably can see where they're building the wicker man they're calling Bogie.

Sharon and Matt descended sideways trying to keep their

balance until they reached a large rock beneath which there were dark shadows. A foreign sound found its way into the crevices of the rocks surrounding them.

"Look, Matt," Sharon said and tugged on his sleeve. "There are some steps cut in the rock to the right. Let's do it."

The steps led down in a steep descent to another ledge from which a rope ladder hung into the shadows below.

Matt, carried by the enthusiasm of Sharon, followed her to where the rope ladder was connected. They could now see where the wicker man stood illuminated like a space rocket prior to launch. Tiny nude human figures holding hands moved around a Maypole in cadence to the discordant, orgiastic sounds of instruments that filled the night like a cat in heat.

"Holy cow, look what's going on," Matt said.

Sharon thought she heard sounds from below the ledge.

"Matt, I think I hear sounds. Let's get out of here!"

As they turned to climb back, a head and torso appeared on top of the ladder. The head and beard had been shaved. The face was emotionless and the lips drawn tight. In one hand the man held a sawed-off, double barrel shotgun.

"You're right little lady," he said in a flat voice, "But you can't. You done seen too much."

THE APE MAN COMETH

April is the cruelest month on "The Mountain." That's what the old-timers say. The snow crust of winter is still on the ground in hidden places as ferns strive to raise their curled heads through the melting mush. Wild animals have a lean and hungry look, and the bleakness of a harsh winter has left its angry mark on the land.

In less than a week residents should be able to exhale as the month of May with its promise of new birth would bring tranquility to the land. But it's not working out that way. There is a pall over the University that doesn't have anything to do with bad weather. With the investigation of the attack on Megan Pappas still aggressively pursued, and a bizarre occurrence at the convent involving Mother Superior Mary Celeste causing rumors, yet another mystery has caught the attention of the campus—popular senior Matt Porter and his sister Sharon have vanished following a late afternoon stroll, and are nowhere to be found. To add to everything else and despite security warnings, Cindy Moses, sophomore biology major and sturdy goalie for the women's soccer team, decided to go for a short hike with friends to collect some specimens for her botany class. Unfortunately, she fell behind to observe a Venus Flytrap about to devour a deerfly that had ventured too close; and it was as if she had been devoured as well since she disappeared without a trace and was not found despite an intensive search.

Frightened parents are now calling their children home until order is restored. A new breed of security with hard eyes and barely concealed weapons patrol the campus in a silent cadence. There is no peace in the land.

If all these bizarre events aren't enough, there is the presence on campus of a character with an alarming visage that has frightened the wits out of the few who've had the courage to approach him.

"Have you met Mr. Pender Hicks," the attractive woman who accompanied him would say. The curious would look down at a creature that looked and moved like an anthropoid, and although bathed, smelled somewhat different also. "God, an ape," the words would form silently on their lips, and then the creature would speak in a modulated voice. "Don't be alarmed by the way I look, and by the way, I'm pleased to meet you."

The attractive woman was forty-one-year-old Doctor Rachel Porter with whom Pender had a unique relationship. She was twelve-years-old when she was kidnapped and taken to a forest hideout by a psychopathic criminal intent on murdering her father Ben Porter. Pender had placed his own life at risk by helping the senator-to-be rescue his daughter from what was sure death, and Rachel had returned the favor by rescuing Pender from a runaway life as a carnival freak.

The way Pender told his own story, as best he could remember it after so many years, he was abandoned as an infant on the county line between Pender and Brunswick Counties in North Carolina "and that's how I came by the name Pender," he would say.

Seth Brown, an old Baptist preacher who found him naked, except for the light blanket that covered him, thought that he was a newborn ape because that's what he looked like covered with black hair the way he was. But being a devout Christian the way Pastor Brown was, he took him home to Mrs. Brown, whom he called 'Mother'. And she said, "Mr. Brown, I believe this is a human boy. Look at the blue eyes and red lips. I don't know that I've ever seen that in no ape."

"Seems that Pastor and Mrs. Brown never had any kids, and being believers the way they was, they took me in and eventually adopted me," Pender once told a close friend. "Old Pastor Brown was the calmest and most patient guy I've ever met, especially with me, the way I was handicapped—that is until he got up to preach, and then he was something else. He would prance around the stage, screaming about the evils of booze, smoking, and women he called hussies. I never saw anything like it. His face would get all red, and he would keep flinging his arms around like he was having a fit or something. I thought he would bust a gasket, which he eventually did. And the funny thing was, all the pallbearers stood outside smoking until it was time to carry the casket in.

"Mrs. Brown, she just fell apart. Couldn't figure out what to do without him. She wasn't that old, but the way she fixed her hair, and the long black dresses she wore that reached the floor, you would think she was a hundred. I tried to hang in and help her, and I did for a while, but it got so depressing with the way she kept mumbling and twisting a handkerchief into knots and wearing that black veil everywhere that I had to move on and ended up in a sideshow at a carnival. I probably should have stayed on longer, but something inside told me it was time to go and it turned out to be right. I heard the women of the congregation embraced her. Even so, when I went back to see her, she was in an institution, sitting on the porch rocking, and she smiled at me like I was a stranger, and when I said 'Momma, it's me Pender,' she just kept smiling."

Pender has not divulged all. His past has encompassed prison, escape, and redemption in risking his own life to save the life of Ben Porter's daughter. It has been a long, arduous, and dangerous road to where he presently stood on a remote mountain somewhere in Tennessee looking down on a hidden hollow where danger was as palpable as sweat on your brow. Unknown to all but one member of a new taskforce created to investigate disturbances in the valley, Pender took it on himself to utilize the only skill he has mastered as well or better than anyone else—in all the carnivals where he would play the part, he was known as Ape Boy.

"Come see the amazing, unbelievable Ape Boy, half human, half ape, captured in deepest, darkest, equatorial Africa," the barker would shout. "You won't believe it folks!" Then Pender would climb and swing in a cage, and he was so convincing that his was the most popular act in the freak show.

As he grew older, he took on different "Ape" roles, changed his last name to "Hicks" for emphasis, and actually got a minor part with one of the big name circuses before he got hurt and couldn't perform. But that was then, and now was now. He was fast approaching thirty years older than his prime circus days, and time had long begun to eat away at his skills and physique. Nevertheless, he felt he had one more "Act" left in him, an act that he was ready to attempt one last time to save a family he had grown to love.

CAPTURING MARY

What do you do when your best laid plans begin to fall apart, when the vagaries of fate slip through the faults in the blueprint of your design like the whistling wind through the drafty mortar holding together the structure of an old house? That was the conundrum Vincent Gower faced as the month of May was fast upon him, and with it the ancient ceremony of the burning of a man constructed of wicker—an event symbolizing the death of winter and the advent of spring. If Matt and Sharon Porter hadn't stumbled on the nude sowing of the seeds ritual around the Maypole, Vincent could have proceeded as planned. But he had received word the Porters had been captured and imprisoned, and he knew all hell would soon break out. He had to strike tonight if his plan was to work.

What do you do when it is dark and windy, and the scudding clouds obscure the morning star; when you are looking at a moat with the bridge up so there is no direct access to the castle-convent?

That's the problem Vincent was facing as he, Maeve, and Sibyl stood together out of sight in the cover of a thicket of young maple trees, and watched spotlights search the night.

In black Army Ranger gear purchased from the Army Navy Store, the three crept toward the moat from the rear of the convent. Vincent had brought a small grapnel with three flukes attached to a light but sturdy rope. They found a place where the moat narrowed to accommodate a wooden bridge, much smaller than the one at the entrance, over which supplies could be brought into the convent's kitchen. The bridge had been raised and secured by chains and locks. Vincent swung the grapnel over his head like a cowboy does a lasso and let it go. The grapnel bounced off the side of the moat. On the third try it found a crevice and was drawn tight. Maeve was the lightest of the three and went across clinging to the rope like a sloth hanging upside down from a limb. Once the rope was tied off, Vincent and Sibyl followed.

They stood facing a locked gate, which opened onto the garden at the rear of the convent. The door locked from the inside and barbed wire covered the arch at the top. Standing on Vincent's shoulders, Maeve cut the wire and dropped down. A few minutes with two picks, and the door was opened. The three crossed the garden to the rear door of the convent. Vincent knew from a newspaper column on security within the convent that there was an iron bar that was slipped in place at night to secure the door from the inside. Vincent had planned the break-in in such detail that he went straight to the wall of the convent, threw the grapnel, caught the last rung of the outside fire escape, and pulled it down. Maeve had her instructions. Up the fire escape. A glass cutter to get access to the inside lock on the window that opened into the hall. Kill anyone that she ran into, but no one walked the floors that night unless there were ghosts, and they were silent.

The three stood in the dark hall with night vision goggles turning their surroundings green. The sounds of snoring and some-one talking in her sleep found their way through the ancient doors like whispers in the dark. Vincent led Maeve and Sibyl down the staircase and to the door of the Mother Superior's room, which was just like others he had seen when he was a priest. The door was locked but again the picks did the trick.

Mary Celeste was sleeping on her back with her arms crossed on her chest. Vincent stood for a moment as if in a trance looking down at her. Even mutilated with the scar descending from the surgically repaired ear to the bottom of her neck, she was still the most captivating and arousing woman he had ever known. He reached down and covered her breast with one hand and her mouth with the other. Mary jerked awake, and Sibyl quick as a jungle cat was on her pinning her arms. That was the sole reason Vincent had brought her, to help him control Mary Celeste. Maeve, he knew, was too volatile and unpredictable.

"Mary Celeste, it's Vincent. Please don't resist. I have come to take you away to a special place where we can be together."

Mary Celeste tried to free her mouth to bite his hand but Sibyl forced her jaw shut and Vincent taped her mouth. A needle pierced her arm, and the plunger was pushed, injecting enough sedative to make her manageable. Now the most dangerous part of all—getting her out of the convent and back to the hidden van without being noticed.

The plan unfolded smoothly—back through the halls of the convent to the kitchen door; into the kitchen, and then to the door that opened to the garden. Remove the iron bar, hurry outside and to the moat. Finally, after fumbling with the locks that secured the small bridge, they led the sedated Mary Celeste across.

All that was left to secure escape was to make their way through the woods back to the van—a good half-mile along a path that was barely distinguishable from the rest of the woods. Sibyl led the way whacking and pushing limbs aside with a small machete.

Vincent had hidden the van where a tractor had started to clear space for what was once supposed to be a picnic area but was now abandoned. The van was parked where the clearing was unfinished so it could not be seen from the road. Mary Celeste was tied to a stretcher. Vincent drove carefully all the way down the mountain highway and along the road that led to the Hollow. Then she was led to a compound where those who were confined there were told to leave all hope behind.

THE COMPOUND

The compound where Matt and Sharon Porter, along with a terrified, sobbing Cindy Moses, are confined is a small, rectangular wooden building. It is dark inside, a naked 40-watt bulb providing the only light. They have talked themselves out and now sit on rusting folding chairs awaiting the coming of dawn and a decision made on what to do with them. They doubt they will ever be freed.

Sharon has been treating Cindy Moses and now has come to sit beside her brother.

"They caught her inspecting a Venus Flytrap," she says. "They took her to one of the tents and assaulted her. She bled pretty bad, but I've got it stopped now."

Matt clenches his fist. "Butchers! Damn 'em to hell! When I get out, that's where they'll go."

The compound is located at the far end of the Hollow's encampment where the terrain rises gradually until it finally reaches the flat side of the mountain. Unless you have the strength, experience, and sophisticated climbing equipment, you will not reach the ridge high above where you can rest and proceed on foot. Against the wall of the mountain incline, a natural fissure in the granite has been adapted into an enclosure that serves as a cell for prisoners who will not conform. The mouth of the enclosure is closed by iron bars with an opening beneath the bars through which to slide food. Water is gathered in canvas bags that have been placed to collect the liquid that continually drips from the sides of the granite walls. Human waste is disposed of in a narrow crack in the granite filled with lime. This is the nature of the judgment those who try to escape will face.

The concentration camp construction is designed to prevent dissenters and nosey visitors from reporting the truth of what is happening in the Hollow. A galvanized metal fence, twelve feet high, is topped by rolls of barbed wire and surrounds the compound. Guards with shotguns and rifles block the only gate, and patrol the boundaries in the syncopated rhythms practiced by ex-military. It seemed so innocent at first—young people, mostly young women, gathering in a valley in Tennessee to have fun and observe the May Day ceremonies and the burning of Bogie. These holdovers from the Woodstock and flower children period couldn't foretell that soon they would be seated on the ground under a canopy of trees being instructed in a pagan religious belief and subjected to mind control and psychological pressures designed to bend their wills into conformity.

In still another room inside the Compound, Mary Celeste lies on a sheet hastily placed on a sweat stained mattress covering a plain unadorned iron frame circa the early twentieth century that has been confiscated from a nearby junkyard.

Mary Celeste is beginning to emerge from the fog of the drugs injected into her hip. Vincent Gower is standing, looking down at her. She has never been as vulnerable as she is now, but he is just studying her in spite of the power he still holds over her.

Helpless, helpless, is her wounded body, stretched out defenseless before him. And yet he just stands watching her as she regains consciousness.

Where is the thrill now? Before, it was always the pursuit and the visceral, overpowering sense of conquest. Now, there would be no conquest. A rather frail, older woman harboring wounds from the past is lying before him. Her skin is no longer the sensual pink that once drove him to distraction. The beautiful strawberry blond hair he once glimpsed is graying and brittle. Her breasts, once full and pushing at her habit are now deflated and empty of nourishment. What is left except only the magnetic pull she exerts on him, only a Druid's death? He remembers the words of the Celtic God whom he called upon when he performed the ceremony Imbas Forosna: "Behold, before you where I am standing is a vision from the future."

The vision he had seen terrified him. The destruction of the present form of his soul was coming too fast. The journey to the Otherworld, where he would be changed and join his most ancient ancestors, was too close at hand. The forces of the present world were closing in. It was finally time for him to act.

Mary Celeste sat up in bed and stared at Vincent. She spoke to him as if he were a child. "Vincent. What are you doing here?" she said.

Vincent's eyes went out of focus. He was looking through her to some place far beyond. "I have come to take you with me to a place where we can be together," he said in a quiet voice.

"What are you talking about?" she asked, her voice now trembling. She realized a spell had come over him. Was it madness?

"Being a Christian, you would not understand. Listen, do you hear the noise down in the Hollow? My people are readying everything for the May Day ceremony, where you and I will preside, and you will dance for the fertility of the crops."

"Let me go, Vincent. Look at me. I am no use to you now. I never was, I am old and my body is broken. I have lost the child you fathered, the child I gave birth to. I have nothing left. Please let me go back to the convent. The sisters need me. You don't. Please."

Sparks seemed to fly from Vincent's vacant eyes. They came alive with a passion that frightened Mary Celeste.

"I'm afraid our destiny is already foretold," he said. "The ceremony will soon start. Prepare yourself to go."

Shadow of Fear

In the woods on the mountain above, a gnome-like monkey figure prepared to climb a tree and swing to a location where he could enter the compound.

PLAN OF ATTACK

The team had gathered. Teams would be the better way to explain the mixture of men, uniforms and equipment pressed into a large Quonset hut at a Tennessee National Guard Training facility near Cowan. Restless feet scraped and pawed at the floor. The assault on the Hollow approximately twenty miles away only awaited the call to action.

The Department of Drugs, Alcohol, Tobacco and Firearms had sent their most experienced SWAT team made up of Navy Seals.

The Justice Department had wanted to drop a team down the mountain from the town of Sewanee to overwhelm the guards at the prisoner compound where Matt and Sharon Porter were being held captive, but cooler heads had ruled it out. It offered too much of a risk with the number of guards positioned there since the arrival of Mary Celeste whose presence had recently been picked up by surveillance craft. The new plan was to wait for the crowd to assemble for the burning of Bogie. At some point before the ceremony it was believed that most of the guards at the compound would be brought forward for crowd control. When that occurred, a lone member of the assault team would be dispatched to secretly break into the compound and free the prisoners. Snipers would take out any remaining guards. Unfortunately, the best laid plans of men often run into a hitch.

United States Senator Ben Porter pushed to the front of a small wooden platform and stood with legs spread and arms extended in a stance familiar to his Senate colleagues. Everyone in the room knew of his valor during World War II, as well as the classic 'David and Goliath' battle in the swamp between Ben, who was perhaps 150 pounds soaking wet at the time, and the monstrous 350 pound giant of a man named Luther who stood more than seven feet tall and who was bent on destroying him. Upon hearing that Ben and Sharon had been captured and were being held, he had flown to Chattanooga and met with the FBI team and the others who now stood before him.

"I want to ask you guys to please use an extra amount of discretion," he said, his voice trembling, something seldom heard from the Senate's distinguished Medal of Honor recipient. You know that my son and stepdaughter are in there, and my sister-in-law, Mary Celeste, from Our Lady of Perpetual Help, is also missing and has been sighted there as well. I would be with you on the raid, but they won't let me go. Please, please, be careful if it comes to gunfire."

A tall, broad shouldered, Native American stepped up on the stage beside Senator Porter, his bronze skin and dark eyes standing out in contrast to the pale skin and blue eyes of the Senator. His name was George Santanta, a descendant of the fierce Kiowa war chief, Set'tainte, called White Bear. The leader of the SWAT team, he had distinguished himself by his organizational skills and coolness under extreme pressure. He was there at the order of the President.

"Thank you Senator," he said as he turned to offer Ben Porter a smile. "We'll take it from here, guys, but the Senator's right. Got a lot of young people in there, mainly young women and people from around the valley. We've got to be careful with the gunfire, but that doesn't mean we have to take unnecessary chances. Okay. We've already covered this in detail and you all have handouts. I'll summarize:

"Our job is to protect the inhabitants and capture this guy— name of Vincent Gower aka Victor Gant. You all see his photo? He's had some work done on his face so take that into consideration. There are some tough looking males hanging out there. Some are guards. We've had an agent in there that says they got guns, so watch out for that, as well. Expect to catch everyone in the middle of a May Day ceremony with a wooden structure resembling a man that they plan to burn. State police here are going to guard all the exits because we don't want anyone coming or going. FBI guys are going to secure the Maggie Bullock's house and the path to the Hollow. The entry to the Hollow is behind the house, and that's where we'll go in.

"One final thing. FBI Chattanooga has something to say. Kay, where are you? And Scarlett? There you are, behind Jeff. Come on up." Kay Steele emerged from behind a stern looking young Navy Seal carrying a sniper's rifle who was known by most as "Z", the initial of his last name.

It was obvious from the greeting that Kay and George had worked together in the past. Quint Parker stood emotionless, aware of a connection from a failed raid many years before. FBI agent Scarlett O'Quinn, garbed in combat gear, stood next to Kay.

Kay managed the platform with a simple hop. Her golden hair was secured in back. She wore FBI's drab assault attire and held a Kevlar Vest in one hand. A Glock 40 Caliber pistol was in a holster on her belt.

"Thanks, George. It's been a while. All right, I've got seven agents assigned to the Widow Bullock's house and immediate property. We've been looking at the house. Vincent Gower comes by occasionally and someone wearing a nurse's uniform, and there's a housekeeper that drops by. Also, they've got guards there. We don't know how many, but our spotter said there were three an hour ago. We've got photos. Gower's or Gant photo is updated on your print.

He's careful not to disclose too much of his face, and usually comes at night so it's a little blurred. When we take down the property, we'll give you the signal on our frequency. Good luck guys. See you at the other end."

Outside the hut, three vans with disguised exteriors were waiting. They would leave at ten-minute intervals to avoid curious eyes and rendezvous at the Hollow at dusk. There would be no nonsense. They were going to take down the site and capture or kill Vincent Gower.

PENDER TAKES ACTION

Pender Hicks followed the tree line, and with monkey-like movements scaled a tall oak. Crouched on a stout limb with his back to the trunk, he was perhaps forty feet above and to the left of the entrance to the Compound. He could see a single guard standing at 'parade rest' in front of the gate. He had also seen Mary Celeste, Vincent Gower, and two other women leave the Compound.

Pender realized that something must have gone seriously wrong. They were supposed to still be in the Compound when he arrived. Sharon and Matt Porter remained inside with another female, but he must act if he wants to save them. The problem is getting to the guard who seems alert and cautious since the departure of the other guards.

Pender thought about dropping to the ground and sneaking up on the guard but the perimeter around the Compound is a problem. A snapped twig, any kind of noise, and the guard would have ample time to react. So he is compelled to find a way from above.

Spotting a small pine tree, not much larger than a sapling, growing beside the gate, Pender made his way there. It is the only tree that remains, and is only there because it has pegs driven into it that hold canteens and other items of use in close proximity to the station of the guard gate. If he could land on it that tree, he might have a chance. Looking at the extension of the limb that he is on, he realizes it is too high for him to jump from. He must get lower. As he scampered down the tree as far as he dared, the guard lit a cigarette, momentarily putting his rifle aside.

Pender hesitated. If he made a wrong move, he would either be dead from a fall or a bullet. His past flashed before him. At the carnival, the gravity defying leaps he made into space with no net below went well until he finally reached the big-time with the circus in Sarasota. Then something went wrong. The partner in the act let his hairy arms slip. After months in the hospital, he was finished as a trapeze artist.

With only the future and the fate of those inside in the balance, Pender stepped out onto a frail limb and propelled himself into space. Landing on the pine sapling, his weight quickly bent the tree before depositing him squarely on the guard. A single blow from the force of his time-hardened clenched hand crumpled the guard. Taking the keys off the unconscious man, Pender opened the gate and rushed into the building that held the captives.

To the cries of relief from Matt and Sharon, Pender cracked a wry smile before glancing at Cindy Moses. At the sight of him, she put her hand to her mouth.

"Have I met you?" he said with a touch of social humor, the smile still on his face.

Cindy Moses issued a cry of relief.

Pender's face stiffened. "We have to leave now. Mary Celeste, you guys, me, we're all in grave danger."

Matt takes Cindy Moses by the hand as Sharon moves forward, her face hard with anger. Stopping to tie up the guard, Matt picked up the guard's rifle, Sharon his knife. Then they disappeared on the trail following the sounds coming from the Hollow, Pender leading the way. Halfway down the trail toward the opening where the May Day ceremony is about to begin, they observe movement ahead. Someone is coming up the trail toward them, someone headed in the direction of the compound.

Moving off the trail, Matt clamped his hand over Cindy's mouth to quiet her. The figure continued to come toward them, and Sharon recognized the man as the one who took Matt and her captive. She saw the terror in Cindy's eyes as she jabbed her finger toward him. When the man reached their location, Sharon stepped in the trail to block his path. A look of puzzlement colored his face, and before he could react, Sharon ran the knife blade between his ribs as she came face to face with his horror-filled eyes.

The man tried to pull the blade out but Sharon wrapped her free arm around him in a bear hug until he slumped to the ground. The group moved on toward the voices and sound of music ahead of them. With a nod, a wink, and a few words, Pender disappeared into the brush. Brother, sister, and Cindy crept forward until they stood in the shadows on the periphery of the circle where the musicians and dancers were ready to perform.

PART SIX

RITE OF SPRING

DANCE OF DEATH

Maeve and Sibyl walked behind Vincent and Mary Celeste from the compound to the clearing and stood in the late afternoon shadows of Bogie Man while Vincent spoke to the visitors and groupies.

"Welcome to our celebration of May Day," he said. "Thanks also to our many friends from the valley that have come to celebrate and volunteered to provide music for the ceremony. Tonight, as is appropriate for a May Day Ceremony, our troupe will perform our version of the Russian composer Igor Stravinsky's composition for the ballet, The Rite of Spring. A few words about the performance to follow: As they should be, our musical instruments are from the valley and surrounding hills. We are fortunate to have horns and drum sections from the local high school band with some other instruments in the mix. Also, we have dancers who will surprise you as they blend into the performance. At the conclusion we will burn the wicker man, Bogie, as we issue in the magic of spring."

Although he could not have seen Maeve and Sibyl arrive, it was almost as if he knew they were there as he turned and beckoned them forward. Vincent handed Mary Celeste over to Sibyl. "Show her how to dance with the group and stay with her until I join you," he whispered, and took Maeve by the hand and pulled her further into the shadows.

Sibyl drew Mary Celeste close so they could speak under the cover of the music without being heard. "Look, Sister or whatever they call you, we need to understand each other. I didn't ask to be here. I got pulled into it. Doing this Bogie Man thing was all fun at first, but then Victor changed and got into all this bizarre Druid stuff. I overheard him and Maeve talking about what he wants to do with you in this dance coming up, and it's plain crazy. It's based on some ballet in Russia where this girl is chosen to dance until she dies."

Mary Celeste gasped. She knew what Sibyl was referring to—Igor Stravinsky's composition for The Rite of Spring concerned a sacrificial fertility rite in pagan Russia where a virgin was chosen to lead the other dancers at a frenzied pace until she collapsed from fatigue and died.

Sibyl hardly took a breath before continuing. "I'm going to try to get us both out of this place, and I need you to trust me and do what I tell you," she said. "I'm going to let go of your hand now and count on you to follow my lead."

Mary Celeste studied Sibyl's face and body language and unlocked her personal history. She was clearly a girl who had learned to act tough to protect herself, but very vulnerable once the façade was cracked.

"You don't have to worry about me following you," Mary Celeste assured her. "The man you call Victor Gant is an insane, defrocked priest named Vincent Gower who is bent on destroying himself and those around him. We must be careful!"

Sibyl released Mary Celeste, and for a brief moment as they looked into each other's eyes, a flicker of terror played on their faces.

From where they stood apart from the group, Vincent looked down into Maeve's face. Her narrow rat-like eyes stared up at him in supplication.

"Please don't do what you're saying," she begged. "You know I can't go on living without you. Please Vincent, Please."

Vincent's eyes and mind were someplace else, but he felt he owed her an answer. She had obeyed him all these years without question. "Maeve, you are carrying our child. If you believe as I do, we will live together again in another life, but in this one, you must raise the child and instruct him or her in our beliefs. Your task now is to get Mary Celeste to the top of the tower with me and then disappear so the police cannot find you. You must escape to Ireland where our people will be your guide and nurture the child in the ancient faith."

Vincent drew a battered brown envelope from his pocket. "In this envelope are all the directions and money you will need. Now do as I have instructed you." He bent down and kissed her quivering lips.

The music and the ritual dance had begun. The steady beat of bongo drums followed by the dissonant sound of horns alerted the dancers of the impending action. It was apparent from the beginning that it would be music of the body, a fusion of music and dancing. A muted trumpet could be heard and the sound of the mandolin floated in the air like a feather caught by the wind.

With cries of anticipation and release, and directed by a dance studio instructor from town, the dancers, both male and female, formed a circle and paired off. Sibyl moved into the line leading Mary Celeste by the hand. At first she moved in a simple dance step, twisting slowly, her arms raised from her sides alternately parallel to the floor and above her head. She beckoned Mary Celeste to follow and was surprised when Mary pirouetted and held her balance.

They had circled the Bogie Man twice to the clangorous sounds of a growing array of primitive and modern instruments and were now behind Bogie where he stood closest to a thicket of willows. Sibyl pulled at Mary Celeste and gestured that they were going to make a break for it. When they reached the thicket they found Vincent and Maeve standing in the shadows. Vincent was waiting with a piece of wood in his hand and struck Sibyl on the side of her head. Mary Celeste turned to help Sibyl and came face to face with Vincent. His voice had a manic intensity to it. "Come with me. You're going to dance Stravinsky's Rite of Spring for your audience. If you stop dancing and protest, Maeve will beat Sibyl to death. You know how Maeve is, don't you?" Vincent led Mary Celeste into the center of the ring and motioned for the group to stop dancing and find a seat.

"Hey, what's going on?" some of the dancers began to murmur.

Vincent pushed Mary Celeste forward. "My lady here is going to do a dance for us," he said. With a twisted smile he hissed in the ear of Mary Celeste, "Dance Mary, Dance!"

He gestured for the musicians to resume, and out came the ragged sounds of the music to the ballet. Mary began to dance, slowly at first and then as the music picked up its tempo, kept up pace until something strange happened. The music seemed to change in tempo with her movements, and Mary Celeste was watched in rapt attention and silence by the crowd as she brought something back from her youth and lifted her arms in rhythm and danced to the music in her mind of Stravinsky's The Rite of Spring. On she danced, faster and faster, lifting her body on her toes like a ballerina. On and on until finally exhausted she began to stumble and fall.

Vincent waited until Mary Celeste was on one knee catching her breath when he called Maeve forth to help him pull her up the ladder into the Bogie Man. Maeve had already set fire to the straw and tinder at the base of Bogie and it began to billow black smoke.

"What?" Mary Celeste gasped. What?"

Vincent almost had Mary to the top when Maeve reached the platform and disappeared down a ladder on the other side. She was gone and no one saw her afterwards.

An expression and mask of madness as if it were fixed in plaster appeared on Vincent's face. "This is always as it was meant to be Mary," he said. "The two of us together forever. I know where that place is, and I will take us there now." Vincent Gower finally had what he had yearned for since his first sight of her.

LIGHT IN DARKNESS

The three buses carrying the agents were delayed by a rockslide as they climbed the twisted road cut into the mountain. Agents hastily scattered to move the debris, but the convoy was going to be late.

When they finally arrived the sound came on loud and clear and the music ground to a halt.

"This is the FBI. Sit down where you are with your hands on your head. You are surrounded. Do not move."

For a moment, silence. Then bedlam. Young women crying. Some trying to pull on their clothes, and get their hands on their heads at the same time. The tattooed muscle men that enforced the rules, sullen, seething, trying to find a path to escape.

Suddenly the clearing was filled with law enforcement personnel: George Santanta, lead his SWAT team into action, sweeping the crowd with their automatic AR-15s. Behind them, the DATF agents infiltrated the grounds, and finally a lone male FBI agent,

Quint Parker, raced across the opening toward Bogie, the burning wicker man.

The last van to deploy held a contingent of Tennessee State Police, local law enforcement and a lone female. Ben Porter, there as an observer, had asked Scarlett to stay behind before she joined her fellow agents.

Ben was exhausted, mentally and physically. It had been a long, long road to where he now stood, and he felt he had to stand erect before Scarlett to deliver the message that had just been passed on to him.

Val Bruce, Scarlett's Godfather, family friend, and legal advisor to Ben's Foreign Relations committee, had called him a few minutes previously.

"Ben, is Scarlett close-by?" Val had asked.

"Hi Val," he'd replied. "How did you know? But I forget. What is it you don't know? She's leaving right now with a deployment team."

"Well for God's sake, hold her there. I've got something to tell you that you won't believe, and neither will she. The search for the files we were looking for on her birth mother, the ones we were told were destroyed in a fire, have mysteriously turned up in a church's repository. Talk about putting pressure on the Church, but I won't hold you in suspense . . ."

Ben turned to Scarlett who had been watching him with a heightening sense of curiosity. What was going on with this usually composed man?

"I need to tell you something," he said keeping his voice flat and unemotional so she could take the news the same way. "The nun, Mary Celeste, whom we know is a captive inside the Hollow, and we all know the story about what happened to her and the child she gave birth to," Ben hesitated while he took a breath. "Well, Scarlett, I have been chosen by Val, to tell you of a discovery just made." Another moment of hesitation. "Scarlett, you are that child, and Mary Celeste is your birth mother."

Scarlett looked at Ben as if he were insane. "What? You've got to be crazy. How could that be? I was told my birth mother was dead, but I just didn't want to believe them. My adoptive parents are my family now." But when she looked into the Senator's eyes, she knew what he told her was true. "I've got to go," was all she said, and jumped from where they sat in the van and raced toward the encampment, the last to enter the Hollow.

Scarlett's long legs moved faster than they had when she was at the FBI training facility, almost stumbling as she raced down the steps into the Hollow. Up ahead she saw Bogie, the wicker man, with fire beginning to creep up his legs. On the platform, Vincent was trying to hold a struggling Mary Celeste. At the base Quint was standing with his pistol, afraid to shoot, and driven back from the encroaching fire.

"Mary Celeste, hold on, I'm coming," he cried. But he wasn't. From where he stood the fire was already too advanced.

Scarlett ran past Quint to the rear of Bogie where there was a detachable heavy ladder. She pulled on it but it would not budge. Hot coals from the fire were at her feet. She pulled again, and somehow the fire loosened the ladder. She pulled it back towards her, jumped up, caught a rung and mounted. She could feel the flames licking her legs and beginning to singe her flesh. She continued upwards until she reached the platform. Mary Celeste was still struggling with Vincent.

"We're going together," Vincent said as he pulled her to him.

"No we're not," she said and pulled against him.

Scarlett came up behind Vincent, and brought the butt of her Sig Sauer pistol against his head. He staggered backwards and fell against the side of the enclosure. Scarlett pulled Mary Celeste to the ladder, but the fire was too advanced to descend. Quint was looking up in despair. He could see the wicker man's supporting timbers beginning to buckle and the structure leaning to the right.

George Santanta arrived and stood beside Quint.

"You guys are going to have to jump," Quint yelled. "George and I will try to break your fall."

Scarlett had jumped from heights during training when agents were taught how to land and roll to lessen the impact, but the tower was fifty feet tall and she knew Mary Celeste's already damaged body could not withstand the impact. The weight of their falling bodies was going to be dangerous to the men as well and end up being a tragedy, but they could no longer wait. Men from the task force began to rush to the scene and stood there helpless with arms extended. Matt, Sharon, and Cindy broke through the startled crowd and rushed to stand as close as they could get to what had now developed into a flame-consumed structure that still vaguely resembled a man. Those closest to the structure began to back away from the heat. There would now be no one to break the fall of Mary Celeste and Scarlett. Quint stood helpless with soot on his tear-streaked face.

Suddenly, a yell from above! Everyone looked up. A body was hurtling through the air. It looked like a monkey swinging on a rope.

"It's Pender!" someone shouted. And so it was. Pender Hicks was swinging on a vine attached to an old oak tree. Swinging was something he knew how to do. He cleared the side of the platform and landed holding the vine. Scarlett reached to steady him.

"Hang onto me," he said as if what was about to happen was an everyday event.

Mary Celeste clung to Pender's stubby neck. Scarlett wrapped one leg around his torso and with the other pushed the three to the edge of the platform.

Vincent was on his feet and advancing toward them, a raw wooden stake in hand. "You can't leave. You cannot!" he shouted and raised the stake to strike.

The fire under Bogie was now being fed by a late afternoon wind blowing through the valley. The supports began to crumble. The entire structure started to tremble as if it were alive.

"Hold on," Pender said, and holding the vine with Scarlett who grabbed it with one of her hands, they pushed off from the tower just as the stake came down, missing them by inches. The three bodies swung in an arc through the fire lit sky. Nearer and nearer they came until they finally touched ground. While trying to keep their balance they were pulled and dragged as if by an open parachute until their momentum was finally stopped by Quint.

Mary Celeste and Scarlett lay next to each other face to face.

"We're safe, Momma, we're safe!" Scarlett cried.

Mary Celeste looked at Scarlett in amazement. "What do you mean?"

"Look at me," Scarlett cried. "I'm the daughter they took away from you. I've wanted to find you for so long." Scarlett's tears began to flow, and Mary Celeste, not knowing what to do, took her in her arms and kissed her. Could it be, she thought, could it really be?

Behind them, Bogie, as if he were an alien shot in war, bent and crashed, flaming timbers and embers lighting up the sky. Vincent's cry was not heard, but he was seen with his arms raised as he was engulfed in the fiery crash. The symbol of death and winter was over. Spring with its promise of new birth and fertility had arrived.

EPILOGUE

THE SHADOW OF FEAR

I am one who has taken fear as a companion. Two manifestations are important. One is how my body reacts at the moment of terror. The other is how my mind and emotions respond afterwards. Some people are gifted with a repressive mechanism that enables them to blot out traumatic events. After a few days or weeks they are essentially back to normal. I have no such ability. I wake every morning to the terror of the past and it is only by the activity of the day that I manage to carry it in the back of my mind. I awoke on what we refer to as the twelfth day of Christmas with the shadow of fear upon me and no amount of activity would let me escape it.

I prefer to go by Mary now although my husband still insists on calling me Mary Celeste when he is trying to make a point. It's okay. I sort of like the give and take we have in our marriage. As a nun, I never contemplated marriage and have had to work hard at it. It's been difficult living outside my vows, especially the sexual part, but Quint loved me and after all that happened I could not see myself going on without him. I guess I'm just a flawed human being after all. We live in the same old weather beaten house by the sea that I brought our child to ten years ago. His name is Bradley. He is thoughtful in his ways and manners and brings much joy to our lives. We have a small garden behind the house where we grow vegetables and whatever will survive the wind and salt laden mist from the ocean.

Quint fishes and we eat a simple, healthy fare. We live a quiet life of thankfulness for the mercies we have received and give back to the community as we are able. We have tried to put behind us the horror we endured, but like a scar you can only hide so much. After all the years of dreading the shadow of fear that one day might again fall upon our lives, we were sure we had finally outrun the possibility of danger from the past, or so we thought. But we were dead wrong!

Our lives unraveled again on January 5th of the year Bradley reached his tenth birthday. We had celebrated the traditional Christmas day with family members who had braved the forecast of bad weather to be with us. Ben Porter and my sister, Sarah, had arrived in his new turbo-powered Beechcraft with gifts for all. Val Bruce and my niece, Sharon, who had gone to work for him had tagged along. My daughter, Scarlett, came with her husband, Jon, and I got to meet my new granddaughter, Portia. Matt Porter, who was working in his father's Senate Office, showed up late with Megan Pappas who had ousted Cindy Moses for his affections.

The following week Quint, Bradley, and I went to the village of Rodanthe to celebrate a unique holiday that is special to the Outer Banks of North Carolina and especially Hatteras Island. It is called by the residents Old Christmas.

Let me explain. For more than one hundred years, residents in this area have celebrated two Christmases—the one that comes with Santa Claus on December 25th, and another on January 6th, also known as Little Christmas, Epiphany, or Twelfth Night. The difference in the twelve days was due to a change by the English Crown adopting the Georgian Calendar in 1751 to replace the Julian calendar first introduced by Julius Caesar. News of the change came late to the remote towns and villages of the Outer Banks. When the residents found out about the new calendar, they complained: "Give us back our twelve days."

The outcome was that folks began to come from all around the island and beyond to celebrate together during the twelve days ending on January 6th. It is said on this hallowed night, cattle come out to kneel and pray, and poke bushes are reported to appear overnight in places where none had grown before.

On this particular Old Christmas Eve, shrimp, fish, oysters and hushpuppies were the main fare along with racks of ribs prepared on a large barbeque smoker. And there was an "oyster shoot" which Quint entered and won a bushel of North Carolina's best. All of these activities were in preparation for the main attraction: the appearance of "Old Buck," the mythical wild bull who ran free and terrorized local farmers and communities until a farmer finally shot him. Today, his spirit lives on in the Rodanthe hummocks and marshes, and he reappears on this night to entertain the children with rides on his back. He is a makeshift horned, masked creature with the body of a blanket to cover the stout wearers who prance up and down with children clinging to their back.

After waiting his turn, Bradley stepped from a stool to mount Old Buck. After Bradley got settled, Old Buck started to mimic a bull coming out of the chute. Bradley held onto the harness and urged Old Buck on as people clapped and cheered for him.

Off to one side was a middle-aged woman looking intently at Bradley. She covered part of her face with her hand, but when she withdrew it, I could see that a tremor had begun to work its way around her eyes and mouth.

"I've seen her before," I thought idly. We had moved onto other things when the realization hit me—that narrow face and the expression of repressed anger. "It's Maeve," I cried and ran to look for Bradley. I found him standing on the side of a dirt road with some playmates. He was watching a car speed away.

"The lady in the green car knew my name. She wanted me to get in, but I knew better."

I grabbed Bradley and ran to find Quint. He was watching a young girl taking her turn riding Old Buck.

"Mary Celeste, are you sure it was her?" he said as I stood breathlessly before him.

"I know what I saw," I answered, my voice rising. "I stood face to face with her when they captured me. She has aged, but I can never forget that face. She is on this island. I know that we are all in danger."

"She's supposed to be in a mental institution for the insane," Quint said. "You remember she couldn't handle what happened to Vincent? And then tack on that the thirty years she got for kidnapping you. She fell apart. Look, I've got to get in touch with the FBI and check it out."

When Quint got off the phone I could see a stern look on his face, one that I had seen before.

"It's true," he admitted. "She escaped earlier today and definitely has had the time it takes to get here. They've put an all points bulletin out for her and for the car she's stolen. The State Police are giving us an escort home."

That night, Quint checked the locks on all the doors and windows, and slept with a .45 caliber pistol within hand's reach.

January 6th, Old Christmas day. Just another day for most. But for Quint and me, it dredged up the horror of events that kept popping up in our dreams and memories to corrode the peace we had fought so long and hard to find.

The day dawned with an overcast sky and a promise of rain to come. Most communications to the island had been interrupted due to a fast moving weather front. Quint ran down to Hatteras village to confer with the Highway Patrol who had already erected roadblocks along the island.

"They found the car abandoned just north of Buxton,"

he said when he returned. Roadblocks are up from Buxton down to Hatteras and they're covering the ferry over to Ocracoke so she can't get out that way. I'm on my way home as soon as I pick up some new locks at the hardware store."

A sigh of relief! Quint was on top of things. I always sit close to the fireplace in the winter when I am knitting. Whether it is my frayed emotions from the past or something else, I can't seem to get warm when trouble raises its ugly head. The heat and the routine had nearly caused me to nod off when I was startled by a noise I heard behind me.

I have always had a fear of peering into shadows, but I turned to look at the far side of the room, which was still just beginning to lighten up. From the depth of the recess a woman stepped out. It was Maeve! I could see that something was very wrong by the way her eyes were hard and fixed while one side of her face was locked in spasms.

"Don't worry, Mother Superior. I'm not going to shoot you, not right now anyway," she said, waving a revolver of some type at me. "Yeah, they thought I was locked up for good, but after all the years inside, if you're someone like me, you can find a way out. And I did. Anyway, see you've got this boy, say his name is Bradley. Wasn't any virgin birth, though, was it Mother Mary Celeste? Guess you broke a few vows tossing in the hay with ole Quint, didn't you? Never did see what he saw in a skinny Jesus freak like you. Guess it takes all kinds for your kind of salvation like that circus ape you brought in to help. Lost my baby in a miscarriage when they dragged me in handcuffs to the paddy wagon. That's part of the reason I'm here."

Maeve brandished a pair of handcuffs in front of my face. "You got to put these on when I say or else I will kill you. Understand the rules? Now let's go see if we can find Bradley."

My life was quickly becoming unraveled one more time. Bradley was supposed to be in his room or the shed out back.

"No, please don't involve Bradley," I cried. "He's just a child. I was on Bogie the day it burned. I'm the one who fought Vincent. It's me you want. Please!"

The gun was stuck in my ribs.

"Move," she said, and we left through the kitchen door and walked down the shell-littered strip towards the beach. We were the only walkers in that isolated area. When we reached the entry to the beach, she ordered me to place my hands behind my back and before I knew it, she had snapped on the cuffs. Maeve led me down an almost obliterated footpath through the dunes. There, in a remote hollow tied to the mast of what once belonged to small sailing craft was Bradley. He was gagged and the rope that held him encircled his entire body. He was helpless to escape.

"Oh Bradley," I cried, and his eyes sought me out. Then something struck me in the head and when I awoke I was tied to the mast with Bradley. Wood from the rotted ribs of the craft was stacked at our feet and stalks of sea oats and dried grass were stuck between them to serve as kindling. Maeve stood where we both could see her. Her face was a mask of hate. In one hand was a gas container and in the other a butane lighter.

"Oh God, no, no!" I cried out.

"Damn you to hell," was all she forced through her chapped, bitten lips and extended her hand to pour the gas at our feet.

A voice came from behind us.

"Place the can on the ground, Maeve, or I will shoot to kill you."

It was Quint. Maeve's hate filled face began to change. She started to back away.

"Put it down now, Maeve!"

Maeve lifted the can and poured it over her head and body. She was laughing so hard she could hardly catch her breath. "I'm baptizing myself," she cried out, and clicked the butane lighter.

Her body completely ablaze, she ran screaming over the sand dune.

Quint charged after her. I could hear her cries from the other side. Time seemed to have stopped by the time Quint climbed back over the dune to cut us loose. His face was a mask of agony. "I tried throwing sand on her to put it out, but it was too late. She is finally out of her misery," he said as he cut us loose and embraced us. On this Old Christmas night, after the FBI, the North Carolina State Police, and the coroner had finished their investigations, and after we had prayed together, Quint, Bradley, and I were in the same bed holding each other and trying to get some sleep when the phone rang. It was Ben Porter. He had been informed and was obviously on top of the event.

"A strange thing has happened," Ben said. "The old house where I was born, and where Mom and Dad lived, burned to the ground about the same time that Maeve died tonight. If you are praying, please pray that the curse placed on our house and family so many years ago was destroyed with it."

Quint and I looked at each other. We realized that we and Bradley were to be included in the prayer. Could the ever-spreading Shadow of Fear that had cast its pall over all of our lives finally have lost its power?

References

What Life Was Like Among Druids And High Kings
by the editors of Time-Life Books

The Golden Bough: A Study In Magic And Religion
by James George Frazier

The Hero With A Thousand Faces
by Joseph Campbell

The Writer's Journey [2nd Edition]: Mythic Structure For Writers
by Christopher Vogler

Past Times: How Outer Banks Carried On Old Christmas Tradition
by Teresa Leonard

About the Author

Gilmer White is the author of *A Time Before the End*. He is a native of the southern coast of North Carolina along the Cape Fear River. He is a graduate of Sewanee, The University Of The South where he majored in English, and after military service studied at the University of North Carolina, Chapel Hill. He now lives in St. Marys, Georgia.